GREEN GIRL

KATE ZAMBRENO

A finalist for the Morning News Tournament of Books
Named one of the best books of the year
by Dennis Cooper at The Millions and by Roxane Gay at The Rumpus

"I can't recall the last time I read a book whose heroine infuriated and seduced me as completely as Kate Zambreno's *Green Girl.* A modern-age Holly Golightly who bleeds Plath and Godard, Ruth drifts through the streets of London in an existential fog, besotted with pretty things and her best friend, at once empowered and emptied out by the desire of men. The skill with which Zambreno inhabits the emptiness of her all-too-recognizable, self-obsessed heroine, clinging to her persona as it turns to dust in her hands, is remarkable."
—Elissa Schappell, *Vanity Fair*

"*Green Girl* is ambitious in a way few works of fiction are. . . . The book is by turns bildungsroman, sociological study, deconstruction, polemic, and live-streamed dialogue with Jean Rhys, Clarice Lispector, Simone de Beauvoir, Virginia Woolf, the Bible, Roland Barthes, and most of Western European modernism by way of Walter Benjamin's *Arcades Project*. . . . A major step forward for a talented and whip-smart writer." —James Greer, *Bookforum*

"It cracks, it zings. It makes you call your girlfriend and read sections aloud over the phone." —Jessa Crispin, *Kirkus Reviews*

"Reading this book is like eating Oreos, if Oreos could be filled with spiders and simultaneously retain their addictive power. I kept opening it, thinking I'd just read a chapter or two, and find myself fifty pages later coming up soaked in the poison of Ruth's life. . . . Zambreno doesn't provide an answer, a cure, a remedy. What she does—better than anyone I know—is hold the mirror up not only to the green girl, but to all the rest of us too: her fatal guides, her toxic sisters, her slavering audience." —Lightsey Darst, Bookslut

"Kate Zambreno's novel *Green Girl*—a finalist in the Morning News's 2012 Tournament of Books—has been almost universally praised in thinky literary circles. It's the story of Ruth, a somewhat infuriating American girl drifting through London, selling perfume, getting drunk, having sex, being beautiful, obsessing over fashion, and struggling to carve out her identity. Ruth is a challenging character and a controversial one—Zambreno calls her an antiheroine, a 'hot mess'—but that search for identity is infinitely relatable."
—Lindy West, "The Jezebel 25: Kick-Ass and Amazing Women We Love," Jezebel

"The best word to describe Kate Zambreno's *Green Girl* is searing. *Green Girl* is a novel about a young woman who is learning how to perform her femininity, who is learning the power of it, the fragility of it. Her education is, at times, a painful one. The green girl is as vicious as she is vulnerable and Zambreno is unflinching in exposing this viciousness and vulnerability in her protagonist."

—Roxane Gay, Bookslut

"We follow both creator and creation through the novel's poetic vignettes—to call them chapters would be a disservice to Zambreno's wonderfully fluid stream of consciousness—as the lethargic Ruth changes jobs, makes friends, takes lovers, and begins to despise them all. Her deep depression and hatred of the femininity she is unable to part with will, of course, bring up comparisons to *The Bell Jar* . . . but *Green Girl* still feels fresh. We can thank the author's unique voice for this, but it is also due in part to the present day setting, which puts forth an interesting question: what happens to women after they've been supposedly liberated? . . . Zambreno's answer is heartbreaking, but as Ruth whines about her coworkers, obsesses over fashion, and finds comfort in *Friends* reruns, you'll find yourself oddly amused by this poignant and thoughtful read."

—Molly Labell, *Bust*

"Kate Zambreno's *Green Girl* is a roar of a novel. It is rambunctious in its language and determinedly off-kilter in its worldview. . . . Darkly exuberant, *Green Girl* reads like tinder, producing a quick and violent burn."

—Anne Derrig, *American Book Review*

"Zambreno's care and diligence for walking the line between artifice and consumption is brilliant here: this is a book I could see savored by both a teen finding great solace in, and someone like myself, who probably could not be more removed from the lifestyle of its matter, who is interested more in how the operation occurs, the patiently squirming sentences hiding and exposing at once what they fear."

—Blake Butler, HTMLGiant

"Without question one of this past year's fiercest texts. . . . As an artist, Kate Zambreno is profoundly non-complacent, and this is the book for all of us ready to confront our own complacency. This is a vital book, a necessary book, a book I will long treasure."

—Tim Jones-Yelvington, The Lit Pub

"Ruth will stay with you long after the book is closed, her shadow drifting down the streets of London, eyes wide, seeking something—forgiveness or acceptance, perhaps."

—Richard Thomas, The Nervous Breakdown

GREEN
GIRL

Also by Kate Zambreno

Fiction

O Fallen Angel

Nonfiction

Heroines

GREEN GIRL

Kate Zambreno

HARPER PERENNIAL

NEW YORK • LONDON • TORONTO • SYDNEY • NEW DELHI • AUCKLAND

HARPER PERENNIAL

This book was originally published in 2011 by Emergency Press.

P.S.™ is a trademark of HarperCollins Publishers.

GREEN GIRL. Copyright © 2011, 2014 by Kate Zambreno. All rights reserved. Printed in the United States of America. No part of this book may be used or reproduced in any manner whatsoever without written permission except in the case of brief quotations embodied in critical articles and reviews. For information address HarperCollins Publishers, 195 Broadway, New York, NY 10007.

HarperCollins books may be purchased for educational, business, or sales promotional use. For information, please e-mail the Special Markets Department at SPsales@harpercollins.com.

Library of Congress Cataloging-in-Publication Data has been applied for.

ISBN 978-0-06-232283-8

14 15 16 17 18 RRD 10 9 8 7 6 5 4 3 2 1

GREEN GIRL

Kate Zambreno

HARPER PERENNIAL

NEW YORK • LONDON • TORONTO • SYDNEY • NEW DELHI • AUCKLAND

HARPER PERENNIAL

This book was originally published in 2011 by Emergency Press.

P.S.™ is a trademark of HarperCollins Publishers.

GREEN GIRL. Copyright © 2011, 2014 by Kate Zambreno. All rights reserved. Printed in the United States of America. No part of this book may be used or reproduced in any manner whatsoever without written permission except in the case of brief quotations embodied in critical articles and reviews. For information address HarperCollins Publishers, 195 Broadway, New York, NY 10007.

HarperCollins books may be purchased for educational, business, or sales promotional use. For information, please e-mail the Special Markets Department at SPsales@harpercollins.com.

Library of Congress Cataloging-in-Publication Data has been applied for.

ISBN 978-0-06-232283-8

14 15 16 17 18 RRD 10 9 8 7 6 5 4 3 2 1

for John

For wherever you go, I will go; wherever you lodge, I will lodge; your people shall be my people, and your God my God. Where you die, I will die, and there I will be buried.

— The Book of Ruth

The pull, the blood, the cry.

The agony of becoming.

I gaze down upon her. She is without form, and void, and darkness upon the face of the deep. Cast in the likeness of her creator. I give birth to an orphan girl.

Now I must name her. Ruth. A hopeful name. No, maybe not Ruth. Perhaps Julie or Kathy. Aah, that's it. Julie or Kathy. No, no. Ruth. She is a Ruth. She is Ruth.

I can't see her. I squint, steady: nothing. I cannot resurrect her. Who is this girl?

I look at a Diane Arbus photograph of a young Mia Farrow. Perhaps this is Ruth. My actress. I try to trace her outline. I learn her curves. The slightest bit of flesh caught in between strap and armpit. The shadow of a line down her stomach, like a bisected butterfly. The slim arms and shoulders. The curve of hair arranged around her breast like a question mark. She is a question mark, a mystery, even to herself. The dark triangle her graceful legs make, toes pointed like a dancer's.

I try to sketch her face, over and over and all I come up with is a furious pencil cloud. She appears. She forms. Yet she is an indistinct blur. She is not fully formed. Dull lines for hair. A furtive little pout. Gray eyes, lead-poisoned. Sad sea eyes. Sometimes an astonishing whirlpool, summer children scampering around the edges, the waters loaded with bodies, bodies, more bodies, their pure velocity forcing through the surface, warding off the evil spirits of change darkening the waters. If only they knew how lovely their proud, brown, hard bodies are, so soon to be trapped inside grave caves of white flesh. Ruth is still lovely as I see her. She is lovely perhaps in her impending decay, like a red rose whose petals are beginning to brown, her last gasp of girlhood. I want her to be young forever. My wonder child, wandering wild.

I am trying to push her out into the world.

The establishing shot.

Train about to depart. Mind the gap. The doors shut like a silencer. Shooosssh. Crowded car. Bodies, bodies, bodies. Ruth remains standing, gripping the metal pole to steady herself. Maybe it'll miss the tracks next time, she thinks. She imagines her face smashed, unrecognizable. Gone in pieces like a porcelain doll.

The tube jerks about on the tracks, like teeth grating. She jerks with it automatically, seeing through into the next car coiling like a snake. More bodies, bodies, bodies.

She gasps a violent inhale. Eyes warm her. She relaxes her face blank.

She leans forward to check the watch of the man reading a *Metro*. The silver timepiece rests on a thatch of black. She is going to be late. Eyes will swivel to regard her as she hurries in to work. Eyes will swivel. Eyes will roll. The terrible girls with their bloodless faces. She will not fall into the pits of their cruel eyes. She gazes at four blonde women, their gold wedding rings clicking against the pole, which they clutch as if drowning. They are wearing sandals and knee-length shorts despite the chill. She pretends to ignore them. She basks in feelings of superiority. She is sure they are going to Horrids. She imagines them ooh and aah at the impressive store towering like a giant stone wedding cake, at the doormen in regal green, scurrying through the revolving doors to become ants in the teem and buzz.

The train suddenly lurches. The four women sway and fall forward. All together. Blonde, blonde, blonde, blonde.

Ruth allows the shocks to jolt through her.

They get off with her to transfer to the Piccadilly, Ruth's face still a cool Noh mask, them chirping, flustered, as they plop gingerly onto the platform. She follows their fat white calves, flaky with dry skin, up the escalator.

Today I must be very careful, today I have left my armour at home.

— Jean Rhys, *Good Morning, Midnight*

Would you like to sample Desire? Ruth smiles at two well-enameled women, their feet shoved into shiny black heels. They glare at her and click past without comment.

Ruth does not depart from her script. Her face smoothes again into her pleasant mask.

Would you like to sample Desire?

An Indian woman walks by Ruth, on each hand twin boys, twin sneakers. She waves Ruth away, as if she was a fly in front of her eyes.

Would you like to sample Desire? She carefully spritzes onto a stick of paper for a bored-looking Italian woman who flaps it underneath the nose of her leather-jacketed husband. Thin red lips almost sunk into her face. He must have to go deep-sea diving for her mouth. She gives back the stick, which Ruth crumples up and thrusts into her apron.

Would you like to sample Desire, ma'am? to an elderly women dressed in bright purple. Bright purple birds nested in gray waves. What's that you say, dear? It's so loud in here I can't hear a thing. She comes up close to Ruth, who repeats herself. No thank you dear, I'm afraid that's a bit too young for me. Again, that pleasant mask. Ruth resists the urge to grab her arm and press into those spots like bad fruit.

A gaggle of London teenage girls, saucily slung things, delicate limbs belted here, flowing there, stomp up to Ruth. Reeking of youth. Can we have some? they demand. She sprays five sticks for them. They gather around the lead girl to smell hers and receive her validation, which comes after a thorough sniff. S'all right. The girls trot away, waving their sticks under their noses.

The girls slinking up the aisles have a rehearsed quality to them, their purses positioned just so on their shoulders, their eyes downcast yet somehow watchful. They cannot escape this self-awareness. They are playing the role of young girls, girls younger than Ruth. Ruth looks at them and feels old.

I look at all of them and feel ancient. (When did I grow old? When did I learn to survey the world through clear eyes?)

A booming voice. Good morning. One of the haughty Horrids heads. Ruth jumps a little. Deer caught in headlights. Good morning, sir, she articulates carefully. The voice comes out little girl's. Her accent makes her appear even more childlike and faltering, her hesitation to say things the way they say them, as they train you to do by failing to understand you otherwise.

She is Eliza Doolittle: Good afternoon, good evening, fare-thee-well. Good morning, good evening, how-do-you-do.

A bit late today, were we? He harrumphs. He always wore one of a series of expensive suits that stretched over his large belly. One of her colleagues, a German girl named Natalie, usually signaled his arrival by miming a pregnant woman with one hand stroke. He would be just starting his third trimester. He liked to perform his morning tours around the departments, straightening a perfume bottle here, a purse there, fanning out a wave of managerial intimidation.

Sorry, Ruth murmurs. She is not really there. Not really there. Best to go blank, to retreat inside. Just be sure to see our un-time-li-ness does not occur again, he hmm, hmm, harrumphs, hand on protruding stomach.

Yes—is all that Ruth is able to squeak out before he cuts her off.

And how are our customers enjoying Desire? In the hierarchy of the fragrance department, Ruth is assigned to the lowest caste, that of the celebrity perfume. She is supposed to shill this perfume by an American teenage pop star with the name that makes Ruth feel a bit demoralized every time she says it. The scent is a waft of innocuous rose, housed in an ornate pink ornament laced with silver and crowned with a pastel-purple tassel. She is supposed to hold it like a chalice delivering holy water to the masses.

They like it, I believe, she responds hesitantly. Sir.

He frowns, his face a placid lake that occasionally ripples in disgust. Maybe we need to mix it up a bit he hmms. Mix it up a bit? Ruth repeats. Yes, try a bit of variation in our language. Ruth does not say anything, playing with the purple tassel on the perfume bottle. He frowns again. He thinks I'm an idiot. He thinks I'm a blonde, American idiot. She mentally steels the tears from her eyes, willing her humiliation into hate.

Close-up on my muse-baby. My actress's face is threatening to turn red, it is twisting. It is not very pretty and reflective as an ingénue is supposed to be. An ingénue is supposed to be ingenuous.

Don't cry. Don't cry my Ruth. Don't cry. You look so homely when you cry.

He snatches the pink bottle away from her, tassel waving. Well, let's try it out, hmmm? He focuses on a gaggle of American tourists, pudgy middle-aged women in pantsuits, shrieking at the vaulted ceilings. Tennessee? Ruth guesses. Texas? Tallahassee? They are like the American women arriving in Paris in Jacques Tati's *Playtime*, riding up the escalator to their hotel with drooped flowers in their hats, descending the escalator with freshly restored flowers.

Good morning ladies, his stern expression relaxes into an almost amiable mask. Good morning, they twang in unison, flattered at the Englishman's attention. I don't know if you ladies have heard, but there's a new product out on the market we're quite excited about, a new fragrance by one of your own. I'm sure you're familiar with? He says the name. Oh yes, my daughter loves her, one of them pipes up, amidst a general buzzing by the group. He smiles without teeth, nodding his head. Well, perhaps you'd like to sample her new fragrance, Desire. It's a pretty, pastel scent, perfect for a teenager or teenagers at heart like you lovely ladies. Well, sure! Why not? Surely! they cry. He passes out sticks as Ruth helplessly squirts a wet dot of rose on each, to squeals and clucks of approval. Well that's very nice. Perhaps I'll get Mary for Christmas?

Let me know if you need anything else, and enjoy your stay, he concludes grandly. The little hen ladies threaten to erupt into applause, as he motions them to push off like children on their first wobbly bicycles. He turns to Ruth and raises his eyebrows, as if to say, See? Look how easy it is. Her lips stay sealed, and curve into her quick smile. When someone antagonizes Ruth, her face only registers a moment of surprise, as if slapped, but then quickly smoothes over.

Be. Better. He waves a fat forefinger at her, and sails off to terrorize Fine Jewelry.

What did that bastard do to you? The German girl, Natalie, clomps up to her. Natalie is constantly getting in trouble for abandoning her post at Molton Brown. Ruth shakes her head, forbidding the tears.

Oh cry cry we want to see you cry. I want to squeeze my Ruth-doll so water comes out. Is that a tear? A tear the moment of truth. A tear in the fabric of the perfected surface.

She feels the gaze of the terrible girls. The tribe of slender mannequins circling in an orbit of feigned disinterestedness, who hawk the couture fragrances. Their leader is Elspeth from the Balmain counter. She is so pale as to be in constant threat of disappearing altogether, her face framed with inky black hair. White and black and cruel. The terrible girls pretend Ruth is not there, although they are always watching her, hoping that she'll make a scene. She is subjected to their constant scrutiny. Look at her look at her my God is she going to cry such a baby has she even brushed her hair today it looks a fright. To the terrible girls Ruth does not even have a name. She is the American girl. She is merely a temporary worker, a status with which she has become intimately acquainted.

Oh, poor thing, Natalie croons. She hooks her arm through Ruth's, her black glossy hair brushing against Ruth's shoulder.

A tear appears in the corner of Ruth's eye. She brushes it away. Go ask Non-cy if you can take your break now. Even though she is German, Natalie is married to an Englishman and talks in a precise, breathy, English accent. She makes fun of the way Ruth occasionally still says Naaan-cy with her Midwestern accent.

Noncy is their floor supervisor, a tiny frazzled blonde who acts like any inquiry or request is just enough to send her over the edge. She is in with the terrible girls.

Ruth shakes her head no. I'm fine. She manages to squeak out. Then insistent: I am fine.

I am fine, fine, fine, fine, fine. The green girl is a liar. She wears the lie on her face. She paints on a smile.

Ruth performs her magic trick of going dead inside.

Lunch this week? Ruth is Natalie's new pet. Yes, lunch this week, yes fine, fine. Fine. How about tomorrow? No, not tomorrow. Tomorrow I have off.

The relief of the end of the day. She can be reborn again, if there is anything left to resurrect. She hurries to the employee locker room. Her purse vomits its contents all over the gray concrete floor. I am a mess, mess, mess she thinks. Exposed tampon like a rabbit's foot. Her lipstick capless and covered with tobacco, like a disgraced crown.

She is such a trainwreck. But that's why we like to watch. The spectacle of the unstable girl-woman. Look at her losing it in public.

Heart beating frantic, she scoops the guts back inside.

She sees the shine of tasteful Italian loafers. Hiya Ruth! Oh, hi Olly. Fingers of red creep up on her face. Olly works in men's neckties. Handsomish. Charming. English. There is something about him, though, something about him, something so terribly familiar... Something about his face... A certain squareness of the jaw... The fleshy underside of his lips...

It is HE who she pines for, it is HE who fills her daily thoughts, buried in between darker thoughts and lighter thoughts. It is HIM who she prays to, offering up her daily meditations. HE is her reference point for everything. She tells herself, she must forget HIM. HE is dead to her. HE has no name. She pushes HIM deep inside although HE often surfaces, on the street, suddenly in a crowd, in a stranger's face.

Need some help. A statement, not a question. Olly crouches down besides her. He is helpful. Why is he helpful? Ruth cannot consider motive. She is otherwise occupied. HE has occupied her mind, colonized her body.

She thinks: *There are strangers here who wear your face.*

Yeah, thanks. The green girl is often inarticulate. Speech littered with likes. She cannot translate the depths. (Are there depths? I am still unsure of her interiority. If I prick her will thoughts rush out or just a mess of heavy confusion?)

Olly hands the purse over. It has no name, the purse. It is black with no name. It looks enough like it has a name, from far away, but up close one realizes the purse's secret, the humiliation of its anonymity.

Good to see you Ruth.

Bye. Feather-voiced. Sending up the American blonde. She is an actress. She is playing herself. She is ready for her screen test. I can think of several blonde Hollywood actresses who could play the part well, yet I do not know their names. They are not as memorable as the classics, Marilyn or Jean, those starry creations that burned bright, died young. I think of young celebrities in the media, stalked by our eyes, the paparazzi, those magazines we read. They exist to draw attention. Aware of the whole world watching. They are green girls too. We give birth to them. Then we destroy them with our insatiable desire to have entrance into their private lives. This is them unmasked without makeup, waiting in a queue at the grocery store, blinking from a sex tape… we watch and watch.

An insight into the lives of countless young women who never knew, or may never know, any other home than the plainest of furnished rooms in a drab hotel.

— Joseph Cornell's notations for "Penny Arcade Portrait of Lauren Bacall"

Three in the afternoon. Half the day buried away. Ruth's days off always oppress her. The realm of choice paralyzes her. To sleep is to choose neither life nor death.

For now, Ruth submits to nothingness. My Sleeping Beauty. She lies in bed still and flat, frozen before an unopened day. Slowly she will thaw. If she moves some spell would be broken. Not a muscle twitches except the delicate fall Rise! fall Rise! of her breath. She has a talent for staying completely immobile for hours, Lot's wife willing herself into salt. Outside her shell she can make out theslamofdoors theblurofhairdryers thepaddingofstrangefeet.

Housekeeping! Thudthudthudthudthud. Ruth resurrects herself. Can you possibly return in thirty minutes? Please? she cries muffled from underneath the enormity of her buried world, trying to mimic the smoothness of normalcy, the Please? ringing out high and trembling. The terror has seeped into the cracks.

No reply. THEY have left. THEY will return. Some days she doesn't let THEM in at all but she has no choice today. She has no clean towels left.

Ruth struggles up and out of bed, capsizing her duvet to the floor. Her bed folds out of the closet. As she swings her legs around to get up she bangs into the chair at her schoolgirl desk. She turns the light on, blinking through her blonde hair. She feels dull. Life-hungover.

Her rented room glares at her with its palette of anachronistic greens—chartreusepuke and another shade she cannot place. Pale cucumber, perhaps? Avocado? Some vegetable?

So this is London. This, this is London. A room with four walls. Four smudged walls of moldy green.

The bedsit is housed in an all-female boarding house near Paddington Station. All foreigners and new arrivals. They travel in cliques divided by country, like the Olympics. There are the Spanish girls flipping dark locks zipping up tight designer denim, the French girls sleek like horses swinging expensive purses, the American girls who strut in tight velour sweatpants Greek letters smacking their derrieres. The American girls who will come home from their time abroad with the itchy vaginas of venereal disease and a life-long weakness for fish and chips. At night Ruth listens with growing hatred to their giggles, to the rumbling of manicured feet, cotton in between toes, up and down the hall, their self-delighted promenade.

It is now 3:30. Her headache makes Ruth feel childlike and melancholy.

In the tiny kitchen with tangerine walls, Ruth pours water out of the faucet into the kettle and makes herself a peanut butter sandwich. She forces herself to eat. She feels faint, not of this world.

The kettle whistles asthmatically while she chews her sandwich at the little sink, staring into an empty alley through the window. She gulps down a cup of tea. The wet teabag in the sink lies there like a dead mouse.

Her head still throbs. Ruth rifles through her purse buried in her bed for her drugs—packages of aspirin, or whatever they call it over here, that pop out through the tin foil. She finds only the shine of empty gum wrappers.

She checks her voicemail, mechanically. No New Messages, the efficient English phone voice. A female voice. Some days hers is the only voice Ruth hears.

The only one who ever called her was the occasional, impatient Hello Ruth It's Your Father. I'm Returning Your Call. Or texts from Agnes, the Australian girl who lives down the hall.

She pulls on yesterday's ensemble pooled on the floor. Hose damp with sweat. She sniffs at her nice black blouse, her only nice black blouse, purchased from the sales rack at Zara. Her nose pricks an overwhelm of worksweat.

Oh to be polished, a seamless image, a film still.

Her mother in her fur coat. Like someone from New England. Regal. Special. Untouchable. Her mother always perfect, an indestructible fortress. Ruth knew all of her outfits, knew their translation. The permanence of her gold jewelry. How cold it was, how heavy, like a lead weight. Her hands so cold. The smell, the taste of her lipstick. She never appeared to sweat. The dust of loose powder. She was allowed to kiss her goodbye, briefly, at the waist, when her mother went out. Never Mommy. She did not want to spoil her hair, sprayed into a helmet, unmovable, the impression she brought into a room. She wished to arrive unsullied. Even when they were in the same room she always appeared like a photograph, a screen of gauze Ruth could not penetrate.

In the aftermath of her mother's death Ruth felt free, terribly free. Like an umbilicus had been snapped. A weird phrase flits through her head. I am an orphan, not quite. Her loneliness contracts, filling her like a well.

Perhaps without a mother one can no longer be young.

Her head throbbing, Ruth stumbles to the loo, as she had started to call it, preferring the elegant simplicity of it to BATH-room or WASH-room. She brushes her teeth while sitting on the toilet, a trickle of warm against her inner thigh, leaning over to spit out the icy blue froth, holding her hair back in a ponytail, taptapping her brush against the sink. Another knock on the door. Housekeeping. The voice is not English. She wipes her mouth with the back of her hand. Just five more minutes! She must put on her armor. She must put her face on.

She gets out her makeup bag, which she rests against the faucet. Her sole purchase from Liberty, with its vibrant print of pinks and oranges. She paints her face carefully today. She paints her own blank slate. The process soothes her. Gray eyes open wide, pouting into the smeared mirror, she powders her face. Swishswishswish. The pale beige powder spills onto the white porcelain, making muddy water when she turns on the faucet.

She paints her blank canvas of a face. Grinning like a grotesque clown, she dips the same brush into a compact of blush—an angry pink—and smooths it on her cheekbones, rubbing away the two mannequin dots that form, up, up, towards her temples. Opening eyes widewider, she applies mascara. The trick is the mascara. She sculpts her lashes. Up, up, up. Her doll eyes lend her the look of the permanently startled.

The final touch. The lips. With a brush, she dabs on the wad of gooey pink lip gloss, the faintest pink, and dots her lips. She looks at the glass. A girl smacks, smiles back. A polished surface. She is airbrushed to perfection.

She looks happy.

Happy. The word echoes back. Happy. Happy. Happy.

She ties on her Sonia Rykiel striped dark blue trench coat (bought with her discount at Horrids), fits her black beret over limp blonde hair hurrying past her shoulders. Her dark uniform. The trappings and suits of woe. As if to offset her youthful glow. Ruth finishes off the ensemble with her black plastic Jackie O sunglasses to protect herself from the glare, of the sun or otherwise. Her sunglasses slide on her head. We see her in profile.

As she closes her door, she sees Agnes coming out of her room down the hall. A girl like Agnes spends the entire morning putting herself together. Or putting herself back together. Agnes does not wear clothes. She wears a costume. Green girls and their costumes, their trying on of brazen identities. Some green girls very in vogue wear cigarette jeans, but girls like Agnes and Ruth only smoke cigarettes. They are the type of green girls to model themselves on *La Nouvelle Vague*, they are new and they are vague. They are the type to wear skirts and dresses with stockings, a specific classification. Today Agnes is wearing a tight cherry-red cardigan and a vintage mustard yellow A-line. A darker mustard trench coat. Enormous sunglasses engulfed her face, as if to cultivate an air of mystery.

Out last night? Ruth asks. A feather voice. She hasn't yet practiced her lines for the outside world. The answer was always yes. She is just trying to make conversation. Balancing her large purse like a piece of luggage (only the necessities!) Agnes rummages around, emitting annoyed noises. Gawd I got so pissed four pints dunno how I got home. Ruth smiles her small way, saying nothing.

Staring into the dull silver of the elevator doors Agnes swirls out her red lipstick, which she strokes firmly onto her lips, back and forth, a brick the same shade as her penciled-in Marlene Dietrich eyebrows, matching her china doll moon face framed by brazenly red hair carefully flipped up. Agnes's hair color changed with her whims, more violent seasons than the city's monochrome. It's my signature she would say. For someone like Agnes it was important to have a signature. How else will she remember herself?

How are the British bitches treating you at Horrids? Agnes smacks her lips together, smiling pleased at herself in the reflection. Shocking things tended to eject from that red mouth. Ruth shrugs. She is a deaf-mute.

Crouching down on her heels out of the Pandora's bag comes large doorknockers that she fastens to each ear, plastic cherry-red the same as the sweater. She crouches down like an athlete in training (no pain no gain!). A bandage is half fallen off her ankle, revealing blood in the cotton, two identical vampire bites above her heels.

The bell sounds. The two girls crowd into the cage. First floor, going down, comes the proper and prompt reply. The sister to Ruth's mobile phone.

Taped to the wall of the lift is today's dinner menu, a haiku of gagging dishes steamed and stewed and breaded that kept the pace of Ruth's week.

Dinner Menu
Curried Chicken
Mashed Peas
Stewed Aubergine
Plum Crumble and Custard

British food was the current catastrophe of Ruth's life. She hadn't eaten a regular meal since she arrived. As far as Ruth knew Agnes did not eat at all, except lipstick and coffee and cigarette smoke. Agnes cultivated a look of old Hollywood, starving her curvy frame into an hourglass. Ruth loved old movies too. She was nostalgic for a past in which she didn't exist.

Agnes begins chattering about a film she has just seen. A Japanese film with bondage. And then it was so BIZ-arrre.... That is Agnes's signature word. Everything to Agnes was BIZ-arre, the fact that Ruth said "candies" instead of "sweets" or "jellies" was BIZ-arre, and Ruth, Ruth was always BIZ-arre. Ruth thinks that the film sounds too gruesome and she wouldn't be at all interested in seeing it, and what's the point, since Agnes had given all the scenarios away. But she stays silent and lets her talk. Ruth tries not to encourage Agnes too much, or she'll be taken hostage forever. But for now, trapped in the little box, she has no choice but to play her audience.

The two girls drop off their room keys in the lobby, to the mournful Algerian receptionist who Ruth shyly smiles at. The lobby is stacked with heavy wooden furniture. Lining the walls are framed photographs of royal visitors stricken with self-importance, the Queen clasping palms with her immaculate white gloves, next to a painting of the place's dour-faced founder.

Outside, London is smeared with a wind-blown sameness. Agnes is still going on and on about the film (won't she shut up?). Ruth isn't listening. She is stone underneath her dark glasses. The gray day has already clouded over her thoughts. And anyway she can't really understand most of what Agnes is saying. Ruth keeps in step with Agnes's purposeful click-clack on the wet pavement.

For some reason Agnes had decided that they were besties, Ruth did not know why, but she did not try to resist it. She was flattered by the attention. And everyone else she had met in London was so clean and dry. Agnes was messy. There were always runs in her stockings, or her clothing was too tight, accidents of white flesh spilling over.

Agnes takes out her mobile. Her fingers begin furiously tapping out a text message while walking. She is a concert pianist manufacturing false sentiments. A novelist of nothing new.

Work today? She finally looks up. Ruth shakes her head. Reprieve, her voice squeaks again. Lucky bitch. Agnes works as a barista at one of the coffee chains on Oxford Street, her apron, filthy with brown espresso smears, usually peeking out of her purse. They are part of the demimonde in London, foreigners working humiliating jobs on the high streets where they are "girls." Shopgirl. Coffeegirl. They are Clara Bow and Joan Crawford flap-flapping about the screen before the Handsome Rich Man (anyday!) comes and saves them from a life of soul-sucking poverty.

Ruth had visited Agnes at work once, Agnes frantic catering to a long queue of impatients, hair held back by a red scarf, plastic bangles from Topshop jangling up her plump white arm. Before the coffee shop Agnes used to work at Topshop but got sacked, for various conspiracy theories Agnes would be all too ready to divulge. Just ask.

Want to grab a pint later? Headache, Ruth begs off. Sorry.

No worries Agnes shrugs although she is pouting with those pretty red lips. You can tell she's pouting because she doesn't want you to forget it. She has lit a cigarette and she has stopped talking. This is her way of punishing Ruth. It's called the silent treatment. Girls like Agnes and Ruth communicate by frozen telepathy.

Ruth now stops to light a cigarette, Agnes reluctantly stops with her, cupping pink hands. She brands Ruth's with the end of her burning ciggie, and there is an intimacy to this. Ruth blows her smoke out into the gray air, watching it intermingle. This is to punctuate the moment, a ritualistic cease fire.

They walk down Edgware Road together. They both stop to check themselves out in the window, maybe to make sure they are still there. They walk past all the wonders of W2 kebob shops, men sucking on hookahs, video rental shops with posters of veiled mysterious eyes, jewelry stores selling rows and rows of gold chains, newsagent placard outside MAN BEATEN TO DEATH WITH CLUB (Ruth shivers), tabloids with screaming headlines a famous movie star who is getting a divorce or adopting a child from the Third World or going to rehab or something.

At night these girls lie in bed and think of celebrities, how beautiful they are, what they are doing at that very moment, what they are like in real life.

Ruth promises again to meet up with Agnes—soon soon. Agnes doesn't walk for long not in those heels they are red and vintage as well she is already wincing she is handicapped by the cobblestones. Ideally she would take a limo everywhere or at least a cab, but she has not struck it rich, not yet, so for now she takes the train. But the town's full of eligible bachelors.

Ruth is heading off for a little adventure on foot. She has decided to walk to Liberty. Liberty is like my Tiffany's, she thinks. She had just seen the film in a matinee.

As Ruth crosses the road, she holds her breath and imagines a black mini-cab throttling towards her crashing into her, crushing her shin bones. Ever since she got to London she had developed a morbidity about being suddenly murdered among the masses.

Ruth walks up Oxford Street, tunneling past tourists pushing in and out of high street clothing stores, past the horns on top of Selfridges, the whiff of peanuts from the nearby vendor, moaning softly to herself. Suddenly she lets out a sharp gasp, imagining a hot knife pushing through her ribcage, as a man in a blue jacket presses against her walking by. She feels curious stares warming her.

She stumbles around, outside of herself, looking at them looking at her.

Sometimes she narrates her actions inside her head in third-person. Does that make her a writer or a woman?

The blonde girl walks all nonchalant down the street, hidden by her sunglasses and wan swing of hair, presumably innocent of swivelling eyes. Zoom in, one might see a faraway look.

In the push of the crowd struck by that feeling that she is entirely outside of herself, only faintly aware that she is alive, moving through this world. Sometimes she is struck by how much she goes through life almost unconsciously. She is being swept along. She is a pale ghost.

Such a haunting, vacant quality.

On Baudelaire's "religious intoxification of great cities": the department stores are temples consecrated to this intoxification.

— Walter Benjamin, *The Arcades Project*

Repent! Repent! drones the street lunatic into his bullhorn at Oxford Circus. He is at his usual perch at the top of the stairs descending to the tube, signaled by the red, white, and blue circular target. As she walks by him she averts her eyes so as not to be trapped within his prophecies. For the wisdom of paltry things, he is saying. Ruth turns on the cobblestones towards Liberty.

Her eyes linger on the roses outside the doorway, lovely lavenders, perfect whites, almost a velvet cream, heartbreaking reds, as red as Chanel's lipstick. Drenched in this lavishness, Ruth feels almost intoxicated with Technicolor, like Dorothy in the poppy field. She sees herself as a beautiful girl smelling the beautiful flowers. She savors in this image. The girl in front of the perfect roses dotted with raindrops. Shiny eyes. Shiny lips. A perfected surface. A cosmetics ad.

Ruth shakes herself out of her reverie and makes a right into the scarves department. Like a museum flooded with light where you can touch and wear anything inside. She finds refuge in these sacred spaces. The rows and rows of perfection, an experience approaching transcendence. Her temple of intoxication. Immersed in the glow of thingness. Everything so beautiful, a beauty so acute it brings tears to her eyes. A little girl in a candy shop (no calories!). She loves the geometry of the rows of wallets in leather goods, separated by every color of the rainbow. The purses lined up like surrealist houses.

She fingers the silk scarves, ethereal butterflies, and picks up a pink felt scarf whimsically looping it around her neck. Pink so pink it isn't pink almost purple. Ruth loved color so much she rarely wore any. Except on her face.

A saleswoman swoops down on her. Very nice, very pretty, she croons. She has a foreign accent. Perhaps from Eastern Europe. She wears a blue silk scarf knotted around her neck like a cowboy. Ruth admires the woman admiring her in the mirror. She is overjoyed that she is kind to her, so overjoyed she is tempted to buy anything she asks of her, just so she continues to talk to her. The saleswoman shows Ruth how to tie it correctly around her neck. Perfect for you, because you're so young, she says. Ruth smiles, savoring the compliment, and gingerly removes the scarf.

How much?
50 pounds. The saleswoman senses, smells Ruth's hesitancy.
Oh, you should buy it. She says encouragingly. She plays maternal. Ruth folds it regretfully back on the table, her hand still petting it like a cat. I love this store, she blurts out to the salewoman.

The woman smiles, tightlipped. She is not as nice anymore. Americans usually do, she replies.

Ruth teeters hesitantly up to women's fashion. Shoppers clomp down the other direction on the wooden stairs, clutching their purple bags. She is aware of the watchful eyes of the pretty clerks, all outfitted in various black frocks and standing in languid poses. They are beautiful racehorses. It is a race they are clearly winning. Despite this evident superiority, they are not cruel to her. They smile. They see her. She smiles back, grateful.

These assaults of casual perfection in the form of the shopgirl. The leggy peroxide blonde with a soft doe face. Everything she wears is perfect—it makes Ruth itch. The blonde seems to have fashioned herself entirely out of a film from the French New Wave. How studied is it? How many hours does she take preparing herself for the outside world? Today she wears a black cape, out of which peek lovely wrists. She could be a model. (What is a model a model of?)

Ruth strolls around the racks, reaching out here and there to finger a pleat or stroke a soft cashmere. She lovingly touches these garments she cannot possibly afford, separated by color like a fresh box of crayons. A shiver of delight with each touch.

The leggy blonde is conversing with an Anna Karina type, hair long and shiny like a shampoo ad. The two shopgirls squeal and look admiringly at each other. They are each other's mirrors. They trade in compliments about each other's daily costume, the false currency for the green girl. I love that. One of them says. That is just *darling* on you the other says.

They are conversing about a film based on a novel one of them had seen. I don't like to read books. They're too depressing one of them says. I know what you mean the other one says.

They are waiting for a woman to come out of the changing room. She is modeling a blouse for them. Not a blouse but a jumper. It is bright blue. The two salesgirls gather around. Arms crossed as if studying a painting at a museum. There is strength in numbers. I love the color on you. One of them pipes up. It is *so* you. The other in melody.

Ruth's eyes lock onto a dress, hanging up on the rack almost insouciantly, so aware it must have been of its hold over her. A little black dress. Everyone needs a little black dress. In every closet there must be that little black dress (do you have your LBD?). It's on everyone's must-have list.

The dress speaks to her. IT says: Those who wear me live another kind of life.

Is that me? (Who am I?)
Is that me? (Who do I want to become?)

The dress is giving Ruth an identity crisis.

She approaches one of the salesgirls, clutching IT. IT sways in response, chuckling maliciously. May I? she asks timidly. Voice soft as a breath. She is nodded into a changing room. Soon comes a swift knock. Come out let us see. Ruth opens the door hesitantly. She is naked and exposed. She allows the eyes of the shopgirls to feast on her. She offers herself up to the world.

The two clerks swarm around. Oh, you look like a little Parisian girl! they purr. Ruth beams, swimming in the attention. It's. . . . One of them pronounces the designer's name knowingly like a secret password. It tells a beautiful story the blonde says knowingly. Ruth lovingly cradles the dress in her hand. For a dress like this she is willing to offer up anything. First-born. Soul. Self.

Although it costs two months of her earnings, she puts the dress on hold, vowing to herself to return to at least visit it again although she knows and they know and she knows they know that she cannot afford it. She hardly has enough money to eat. But who needs to eat when you can wear a dress like that? Ruth thinks. Anyway, food gets digested, food goes away. Useless practice. But a dress like that will be forever. A sort of spiritual nourishment, just as fundamental as eat and roof and breathe.

Her perpetual list of wants and can't-haves. To want. To lack. To have a hole.

She is enflamed with Desire. Oh, the pain of true love. She deceives herself that this is what she needs to be complete.

She hears a voice from deep within. The arsenal of voices telling her to buy the dress. Buy it don't think. Buy it. Buy it. It is so you. It enhances your personality. It makes you more you than you were before.

But it is an impossibility. Oh she aches she aches her soul aches. She walks out feeling like a shadow of self, shabby, ugly. Oh, the hunger, the hunger. My hunger artist. Always starving herself.

My hunger artist her art is herself she is fast fasting away she would like to disappear.

Why shouldn't the *flâneur* be stoned?

— Gail Scott, *My Paris*

Stumbling outside, Ruth is hit with the cold and the swirl of the crowds. She hears the preacher again.

For the witchery of paltry things obscures what is right, and the whirl of desire transforms the innocent mind.

He is quoting from the Book of Wisdom. Wisdom is not something the green girl possesses in abundance. Her sacred scriptures are new wave films and fashion magazines.

Walking past Carnaby and down Oxford again, it begins to rain. She doesn't really notice, except for tourists jerking about into the Boots to purchase umbrellas. The clang clang of the Hare Krishnas approach, playing their instruments, chanting their Hare! Hare! Krishna! towards their temple near Soho Square. The rain, which spots their melon-colored robes with translucent patches, doesn't slow them down.

They always look like they're having a lot of fun, Ruth thinks, and stops and claps her hands as they pass by. She makes eye contact with a boy about her age. He grins back at her as he dances around in a circle, his short rough ponytail swaying. She admires the intricacy of the bright white markings like an eagle's beak. She temporarily forgets herself. So ecstatic. So lost inside themselves. So taken up by the crowd.

She jerks and pushes and pummels her way through the throng. Freezing rain. The umbrellas hunched over, protective. Thump of dance music outside the high-street shops. Mannequins. People. You can tell a tourist because they always look up, she thinks. Londoners stare ahead, or to the ground. Not that Ruth is a Londoner but she isn't a tourist either.

Faces here like faces there. Faces and faces. She thinks she sees HIM in the crowd. She is always posed for seeing HIM, even across the world. Perhaps a narrative plays out in her head as the rain stains her. HE has stained her. She will spy HIM in the crowd, no, HE will spy her first, and HE will see her anew. That is why she left, why she went to London. For HIM to follow her here. For HIM to realize HIS love for her and HE is searching, searching, searching for her. She walks as if HE is watching her. She is always being watched. She is not free. The vision of HIM follows her everywhere.

Phrases flit through her head. My mad girl's love song, a hymn of HIM:

This is strange to think perhaps but if I saw you would I know who you were you could be hidden like a stranger in a crowd the Greeks thought that strangers could be gods in disguise are you my god in disguise? Would I recognize you? How could I not recognize someone who so regularly occupies my thoughts? Perhaps now you have facial hair (did you have facial hair)? I close my eyes I attempt to resurrect you conjure you up I can't make you out for the life of me maybe you are not you. Maybe you are someone else.

The green girl is infused with Desire.
Obsession—*Parfum pour femme.*

She shakes her head no at the fliers thrust at her, like a parade of flying legs in a variety show, except clothed in gloves and coupons for Sainsbury's. Sometimes it is easier to just take the flier thrust at you rather than go through the motions of mumbling no, no thanks, although Ruth has learned to blow right by them, rehearsing the same cool look of decline that she has come to know as English in nature. She shakes her head no, doing that quick smile where she doesn't show any teeth. There's the smile, now it's gone. A grimace, not really a smile at all. There was a meaner version as well, practiced on those who did not take the first hint, who gathered closer, urgent and insistent.

Down Charing Cross, past red phone booths with the faint waft of men's genitalia littered with escort calling cards, postcard Sirens luring in men walking by. Ruth shivers. She wonders what it would be like to prostitute herself. To be a beautiful young girl fed to the lions. Like a sort of martyr. Sometimes she fantasizes about this. A state of utter depravation. Except it is a Hollywood version she dreams of, like Jane Fonda in *Klute.*

She prays to be preyed upon. She is a deer standing in the middle of the forest road, knees buckling, begging for a predator. And Bambi has no mommy. The mean hunter has a sexy glint in his eyes. This is why she cannot forget HIM. HE was not fooled by her face of innocence, by her pale pinchedness. HE used her and abused her and she begs for a repeat of this experience. When HE would come over for their nocturnal couplings she would plead for HIM to destroy her, murder her, pound her back into the nothingness from which she began and to which she knew deep down she would inevitably return.

She hadn't known she had desired a beast. Someone to destroy her.

That first meeting ended in bruises that she would lovingly watch yellow over the weeks.

The rain lets up. It will descend again soon. She wanders down the cobblestoned streets of Soho, past the dark sticky alleys of peepshows girl mannequins blankly bearing whips naked boy mannequins wearing plastic grins holding hands of other boy mannequins. Glass windows revealing rows of pastries crowned with whipped cream.

She walks past a shop she had worked at when she first came to London. Ruth had liked the idea of working in a sex shop, the vulgar aspect of it. She liked to slum, to place herself in humiliating circumstances. She didn't know why. The work itself was rather dreary, shelving bottles of lubricant, lining up dildos like wriggly, neon soldiers, picking up handcuffs from the floor, ringing up meekish customers, alone or in pairs.

The manager at the sex shop gave Ruth the creeps. Thin, oily, folded into a crisp suit, a handlebar mustache tickling tight lips. When he walked her around giving her the tour, he seemed to get satisfaction out of trying to shock her. Does it bother you to look at this? He would point to a TV monitor showing a long black penis sliding into a gaping red hole, in and out, in and out. A headshake no. How about this? A phantom penis ejaculated like splattered candle wax over a brunette's massive breasts, as she groaned and writhed about. Trying to shock the American girl with the innocent face and the little girl voice.

We'll try you out he had said to her. As if he was a pimp and she was a prostitute. We'll try you out. A trial period. We'll see if you like us and if we like you. That's what they always say—but what they really mean is we'll see if we like you. The part about you liking them is actually immaterial. And one learns not to care. One learns to deaden oneself and to hold one's breath and wait until it's all done with. This is Ruth's philosophy for many aspects of her life.

She had lasted at the sex shop for two weeks. She hadn't even picked up her paycheck. Ruth had a talent for quitting jobs. Often she would simply not show up, and then they would call and call and she would erase and erase the urgent where-are-yous. She has even been known to just walk out. Oh, the freedom of just walking out, the no-thanks, the not-for-me, the push of the door and pull back into herself.

What I am writing is something more than mere invention; it is my duty to relate everything about this girl among thousands of others like her. It is my duty, however unrewarding, to confront her with her own existence.

— Clarice Lispector, *The Hour of the Star*

Dreaded Saturday crowds. The grandiose door spits shoppers in, spits shoppers out. They are indistinct. They come in waves. An exodus of the masses.

Walking down the row women poised like flierers handing out scented sticks of paper.

Desire? Care to try? Desire? Desire? Plastered smile, pink ornament of pastel scent at attention. Ruth does not even register the constant throb of gloves and shoes and clipping walks. She feels the pastel globe weigh on her hand. It is covered in silver netting, which pierces her palm.

She has to display this bottle of perfume at chest height for an indeterminate period of time, like those Vanna Whites displaying prizes on game shows, a spokesmodel who only has one line to speak, until the powers-that-be allow her to take a break, where she will escape to the employee toilet and lock herself in a stall of porcelain white, feeling the silence of her own breath.

To last throughout her shift she escapes outside of her body and lets it do all the work. She asks woman after woman, all strutting by like robins in their winter wear, if they would like to sample

Desire. Desire? Desire? She is on repeat. The silver is starting to wear off, sparkly silver on her hands, the glitter buried deep in her palm. Angry women swinging their angry purses. Holding the hands of British children, freakishly precocious like tiny adults.

Sometimes she is struck by the sense that she is someone else's character, that she is saying someone else's lines.

At the end of her day her throat is dry from her constant spiel. Her feet and her calves ache from standing. Her cheeks ache from pretend smiling. The very top of her second finger on her right hand, the uppermost joint, aches from pressing up and down, up and down.

Point. Squirt. Hand. Point. Squirt. Hand.

(My Ruth. I write on her bored.)

The piped-in sounds of pop music. Manufactured, packaged, digestable. A song by the starlet whose perfume she's shilling. Cooing sultry come-ons, breathless promises. On a track, repeating over and over again. The landscape of shopper's ringtones. Music that's not music. The buzzing and the coo. Ruth has swallowed all of these noises. She doesn't even notice them anymore.

The horrible head sometimes walks by and snaps his thick sausages in her face. Look alive. He doesn't even say her name. She is nameless. She is an unknown. He had begun to walk by her station just to see whether she was awake, to the delight of the terrible girls. You should be offering Desire to everyone who walks through that door. He points at the door, and then points at the globe carelessly cupped in her hand. The world that exists inside her sweaty numbing palm.

You're a salesgirl. You're supposed to be selling. Are we clear? Ruth smiles blankly. In a fog. Not there. Not really there. Watch her, he points at Noncy, who throws up her hands at him. Ruth imagines her pulling him aside. Those temps, they're not too bright you see. They're only temporary.

Poor Ruth, parroting away like an automaton. Ruth feels tremulous handing out the sticks of scented paper, uncertain, passive. Desire, would you care to? Desire?

She is now supposed to squeak out, Have you ever experienced Desire? The horrible head recently came up with this. But she only does it when he is around, watching her.

Have you ever experienced Desire?

During dead stretches of time she fantasizes about the past the forbidden.

I can see us, fighting like wet cats, clawing at each other, on the street unable to help ourselves, in front of your car, you unable to drive away, in bed at the latest hour, the birds beginning their appeal, knowing the next day to be already ruined. We would suck on each other's mouths as if to drag the life from each other.

The green girl necessarily pines for the past, because the present is too uncomfortable to be present in and the future, unimaginable. The need to long, to desire that which she cannot have, that which has eluded her, because she deceives herself that it was this person, this chance, where she would have found happiness. It would have been this boy, this ordinary boy with his ordinary cruelty, who would have unlocked the key to herself, a self mysterious even to her. The One and there is only ever One so if you missed out, sad for you.

I can see you, red chapped elbows propped up against my pillow, cigarette between lips like a bemused farmhand with his blade of grass.

Have you ever experienced Desire?

She felt ridiculous saying this, like she should be selling herself on late-night TV.

Their job was to sell, sell, sell. There was no official script, officially. All in the delivery. Forceful, yet knowing when not to push too hard. Tell them whatever they would like to hear. The best salesgirl is a liar. The best salesgirl talks a fast game, and isn't afraid to switch tactics when it isn't working. The best salesgirl sizes up the customer and feeds their ego.

would you like to try?
you won't regret it
just a second of your time
you look lovely today
it's a lovely scent
a brilliant fragrance
brilliant brilliant

now take a deep breath
let it draw you in

it's a bit fruity, isn't it?
flowery
so pretty and so French
musky
peppery

quite sensual don't you think
warm and spicy and Oriental
an elixir for the senses

it's a greener note
do you smell the licorice?
you just want to eat it don't you?
and guess what? no calories!

but if you really want it to last you're going to have to layer it you know
oh, you must layer it
do you layer?
first the shower gel
then the soufflé
feel that how creamy indulgent
indulge yourself
then the perfume
make sure to spray it on your errr-ahh-jenus zones

it will never leave you
it will linger with you all day
when he smells this he will remember you
always
in another country
years later

it will be your signature scent
it isn't just a perfume but an identity

a woman's pure essence
found in an oval-shaped bottle

mimicking her curves

for the woman who
wants love
is playful
is sexy
wants it all
has a strong sense of self

it's so classic!
timeless!
it's so modern!

the embodiment of
femininity
old-fashioned glamour
audrey
katharine
sophia
marilyn

this is the fragrance for the
trendsetter
the intellectual
the person who loves beauty
who loves little children
who loves animals
sweet things
sex

who loves to fall in love
who wants to be young

who wants to be sophisticated
who wants to be noticed
across a room but not smelled, more like sensed

It was all porn for impressionable women. Beyond the talk of top velvety notes and powdery cores and layering. The fairytale drivel, the poisonous romance narratives. Peddling in clichés. A love potion of sweet temptation. A fantasy of indulgence. Cue the symphony, the sunset as the backdrop for lovers. Or perhaps you'd like an essence more mysterious. The kind that's subtle. That lingers in the room after the lady has left. A passing moment. A memory. A story.

It comes in a bottle and it tells a story. Put it on my Visa.

You speak like a green girl, unsifted in such perilous circumstance.

— Polonius to Ophelia in *Hamlet*

So, I took another pregnancy test. Natalie leans in closer to Ruth, so close that Ruth can see her black lacy bra. Negative, thank heavens. Her breath smells like tuna. Every day at 1 pm Natalie goes to the sandwich place across the road, to get triangles of mushy bread with ominous fillings. Half-off between 1 pm and 2 pm. Egg pickle with rocket, egg mayo with rocket, tuna mayo with rocket, prawn mayo with rocket. Ruth fights the urge not to gag. Even though they are alone in the employee room, Natalie is practically sitting on Ruth's lap. Ruth keeps attempting to pry herself away, although bit by bit, so as not to appear rude. The passivity of the green girl masquerades as politeness.

Aren't you on the shot? Ruth asks. By now she is intimately acquainted with Natalie's reproductive regime (which usually required total-if-not-complete abstinence). Natalie's voice drops to a conspiratorial whisper. She leans in closer, her pendulous breasts pressing against Ruth's arm. Her chest powdered with scented silver glitter. Yes, but my hubby and I had sex, lower whisper, two weeks ago and I haven't gotten my thing yet. Ruth has seen Natalie's husband come to collect her from work, a goofy tower of Englishness. Are you late? No, no, not yet. I just get soooo scared.

If I got pregnant I would absolutely die. Just shrivel up. Her thickly coated eyelashes tick like the hands of a clock.

Just then, the door opens. It is Olly from men's neckties. He nods at Ruth and Natalie. Hello ladies. Hiya, Olly! Natalie calls out gaily. Ruth smiles, blushing a little, lowering her eyes modestly. She can feel Natalie watching her.

Olly pours hot water into a paper cup.

Going out for a pint Sunday?

Ruth realizes he is addressing her. Yeah…I don't know….But she does know. Although she doesn't know if she is being coy or still being polite. Every Sunday night the fragrance department goes to the local pub for a drink. Ruth has never been invited, since Elspeth hates her. Maybe. I don't know, she falters.

Oh. Well. It'd be nicer if you came along. He finishes his tea, crumples up his cup, and throws it into the bin all in one gallant gesture. All right. Bye now, ladies.

Bye, Natalie says frostily, miffed not to be included in the exchange.

Bye. Ruth's comes out unintentionally breathy, again, as if she were flirting.

Once Olly has left Natalie slaps Ruth's pantyhosed thigh. Ruth winces. Ouch.

You fancy Olly, she says accusingly. She is still whispering, even though they are once again alone. Me? No. Ruth tries to blow this off, like the thought is ridiculous.

There are strangers who wear your face. Is this some plot, or is this my vile hallucinations? I cannot seem to shake you away.

Well, he seems to like you. Natalie appraises her.

Yeah?

Why not? You're a cute girl. She says this almost reluctantly. She scrutinizes Ruth. We're all cute girls in fragrance.

Natalie checks the time on her mobile. I want to grab a quick ciggie before we have to go back on the floor. Want to come? An offer that is not actually an offer. There is a certain area out back on the dock in goods receiving where the terrible girls smoke on their breaks and spray acid on everyone else in the store. Ruth knows that she would not be welcome. She shakes her head no, thanks. She is suddenly on mute. Natalie shrugs again.

As she opens the door, Natalie looks like she is struggling over whether or not to say something. The gossip in her wins out, drowning whatever else was in her underneath the surface. You know, Elspeth fancies Olly. The inferred sign posted on recently wiped glass. Ruth knows this. Everyone in all of Horrids knows this. Last month she bought him a cake for his birthday (dark chocolate), which store employees were selectively invited to eat out in the break room. Ruth had not been invited.

Oh well, she can have him, Ruth blurts out. But then as soon as she says that, she wishes she hadn't, because it was not nice. But she had not wanted to be nice, but she feels ill not being nice. Natalie regards Ruth coolly again. Anyway, I just thought you might like to know. And then she is gone.

Thanks, smirks Ruth, once alone in the room, knowing that in the next ten minutes Elspeth will be given even more fuel to hate her. That American temp, that American temptress, making off with one of their own.

Gossipy Natalie. Like a child who likes to light fires, just to watch them burn.

Ruth is hit again with the desire to swallow her tongue, to swallow, swallow her tongue.

Later in her shift, Ruth's stomach begins to churn, from the nauseating combination of sweet smells and body heat as well as the casual cruelty of it all. She has a fire-breathing belly. A seething sputtering ball of stress. A volcano spilling over messy anxieties, sensitivities, fears. What if it is an ulcer? Ruth worries, worries, worries, while her stomach twists, twists, twists.

Ruth hurries up to Noncy. I have an upset stomach. Fine, fine, *Ruth*, Noncy waves her away impatiently. The way she pronounces Ruth's name comes out as an accusation. She knows that she is daily supplying material for the terrible girls to torment her with. She knows that every move she makes is documented, is reported back to Elspeth. She is overdocumented but intimate with no one.

She hurries to the employee toilet. She locks herself in a stall and begins to explode, emptying out all of her insides. Amidst the horrible sounds and the stink, the outside door opens. Ruth had forgotten to lock it. It is Elspeth and her constant companion, Sam, a watery-eyed Scottish girl who sells Hermès. Together with Elspeth's ghost complexion and Sam's pink and blonde squatness they resemble Roald Dahl's two greedy aunts. Ruth frantically tries not to make any more bodily sounds.

She is in fact the subject of their conversation. Something, something, that American girl. Haughty Elspeth. Something, bad? Sam. She smiles too much. Elspeth. Do I? wonders Ruth, her stomach doing contortionist tricks. Americans, something. Sam. Something, nauseating. Elspeth. Would you like to sample Desire? Elspeth again. Giggling. They're mimicking me, Ruth realizes with horror. The brushing of hair, the blowing of noses, the clasping closed of compacts. The door swings shut.

Ruth is going to be late coming back from her break. But she is frozen on the toilet bowl, skirt around her ankles. Tired from holding it all in, in that stall she thaws. The tears pour out, along with seemingly everything else.

My ice girl. I carve her into a swan.

Before getting on the train to go home that evening Ruth stops at Boots. In the pharmacy she picks up a pamphlet for ulcers, stationed next to the pharmacist, as well as pamphlets for: appendicitis, migraines, tension headaches, upset stomach, irritable bowel syndrome, panic attacks, stress, and urinary tract infections. Suffering from ulcers? a drawing of a woman, hand on stomach, doubled over, mouth curving down, the pain drawn in lines on her forehead. Peptic. Duodenal. Gastrointestinal. A burning feeling in the stomach area. A gnawing. A hole.

The train rumbles past, stopping a distance away. Her reflection multiplies endlessly. She sees herself passing by, staring, staring into space.

Once I feel myself observed by the lens, everything changes: I constitute myself in the process of "posing," I instantaneously make another body for myself, I transform myself into an image.

— Roland Barthes, *Camera Lucida*

Sometimes after work she takes a bath and watches herself in it. Sometimes she forces herself under water. She pretends she's dead. She pretends she has drowned. She is Millais' Ophelia floating down a stream, clutching flowers. The painting hangs in the Tate Britain. Although Ruth has not gone to the Tate Britain. She wouldn't know the first thing about how to get there.

After her bath she gazes at herself in the mirror. Is this what I look like? She marvels at the stranger in the mirror. The stranger looks so solemn, so serious. She smiles. The stranger smiles back.

I too study her, a curious object. Like a prickly piece of fruit. I experience horror at my former self. Is that me? Can't be me. Can't be me. Can't be. I was never that young. Never, never that young. No longer joy meets my eyes when I gaze into the mirror. That me is no longer. She is dead. Dead and gone. Dead and gone. Gone. Gone. She is gone. I have mourned her. I have murdered her.

Later, when we look back at ourselves, we marvel at our emptiness, our youth. The shiny surface. We forget the confused upheaval stirring deep within back then, a revolution that we stifled daily.

There is some gap in between. Some dark hole in the center of Ruth that is not reflected in this mirror. She mutes this violence and turns it on herself. She resists the urge to peel off her skin. Sometimes she would like to put her fist through a window, but she is too well-behaved.

Everyone always tells her how pretty she is. You're so pretty, they say. It is a fact. She could be described in the language of growing things. She is a tender sapling. She is green, she is fresh (yet the freshest ingénues can carry with them the most depraved resumes).

Yet to be beautiful, fresh, young is a horrible fate if one feels empty inside. That is why these ingénues try to soil themselves. No one wants to be a cosmetics ad when depressed. When Ruth is feeling her emptiest, the empty compliments keep on pouring in. She craves the attention but grows nauseous.

She is anointed daily with these compliments.

You have a beautiful smile.
Eyes lowered, the modesty of a saint. Thank you.

What wonderful eyelashes you have.
Eyes lowered, again. Thank you.

She is a willing accomplice to this farce. She paints on the smile. She paints on the happiness. She paints on the natural, glistening glow. She blots a pink heart on the tissue—the pink heart that is her heart of darkness.

The awareness on the train, the fashion show. The men are always looking, always looking with their flirty eyes. One can shop but one does not have to buy.

But sometimes life in the spotlight can be difficult. Sometimes she wants to be invisible. Sometimes walking down the street she sends out signals of distress.

Look at me
(don't look at me)
Look at me
(don't look at me)
Look at me don't look at me look at me look at me don't look at me don't
look
(Look)
(Don't look)
I can't stand it if you don't look
Look
Look
Please
Stop

To define myself in one word: indifference.

— Marina Vlady in Jean-Luc Godard's
Two or Three Things I Know About Her

Ruth is in bed, flipping through American *Vogue*. She gazes at a spread with one of her favorite new models. Recently she has cut all of her hair off, which makes her look reckless and free. Ruth has stared at her picture so many times, cavorting on a safari in Africa, twirling around in the season's new dresses, she feels she knows her intimately, like she is another self. It is again the season for a woman with a strong identity, the magazine tells Ruth. Could she, did she have it in her to update her visual sense of herself? She sits there worrying about this, about the face she puts out into the world.

Moments ago she was on her stomach distractedly rubbing herself against the mattress. When she masturbates the face she usually conjures up first is her own. In her fantasies she is beautiful, more beautiful than what youth naturally lends her. But not only is she beautiful, in her fantasies she is beautiful through another's eyes. Her fantasies are of being witnessed, of being watched. By HIM, the one she must banish from her thoughts but that she allows to star in these fairytales. She can feel his gaze upon her. But today she tries not to think about HIM, she thinks about Olly, with HIS face, or maybe the reverse, trying not to think about HIM so making HIM look like Olly.... It wasn't working. The only way she could get off, could ride herself to ecstasy dry humping herself on her bed was to resurrect the past starring HIM her episodic Lazarus, peeling off the Olly mask, yes it was HIM, HIM, HIM, gazing at her face like it was composed of stained glass, she allowed herself to remember his face, just one last time, but she was having trouble recalling it exactly. And if she remembered his face, if she could only remember his face…

She groans and rolls onto her back and picks up the magazine, lying underneath her.

Knock on the door. Insistent.

Come in. Feebly. It is Agnes, with her red lips still on, wanting to hang out.

They are in Agnes's room. They sit on Agnes's bed. Agnes's walls are plastered with actresses. Monica Vitti. Hanna Schygulla. Corinne Marchand. Anouk Aimée. Rita Hayworth. Agnes's makeup kit is strewn across the bed. Ruth is trying on a dark blood stain, which she thinks with her pale hair lends her a definitive Greta Garbo appeal. She admires her strange red lips in Agnes's large mirror propped up against the bed, pursing them, pivoting her pale chin from side to side.

What do you think?
A demonstrative head shake from Agnes. Not you.

Ruth sighs, wipes with the back of her hand, and against her better judgment begins to confide in Agnes about the scene with the terrible girls in the toilet.

I mean, do you think I smile too much? She asks. She frowns, then smiles widely in the mirror, showing all teeth (are they too yellow?). She salutes herself, as she has seen Jean Seberg do in *Breathless*. She waves like a beauty pageant contestant.

Agnes considers this. Yeah, maybe. I don't know.

Ruth is dissatisfied with this answer. She frowns in the mirror, but it is a watched frown, a measured pout. She observes clinically her furry upper lip, the tiny whiteheads around her eyes, the broken blood vessels around her nose, the scatter of red bumps on her chin.

Anyway, you're really sensitive, you know. Ruth watches Agnes apply black liquid eyeliner, swooping up like cat's claws. Glaring haughtily in her compact mirror.

Am I sensitive? I don't think I'm too sensitive. Ruth studies herself in the mirror. She scratches away the yellow gunk in the corner of one eye.

No, no, you are.

What do you mean, exactly?

Well, it's like, you feel things really strongly, and you can see it on your face.

Oh. Ruth concentrates on a lip gloss. The same moment of hurt, then smoothed over like a shovel on wet sand.

I mean, fuck, who cares? Says Agnes. Who is now looking at Ruth looking at herself in the mirror.

Are you mad? Agnes asks but the way she asks seems to imply that Ruth should not be mad.

Ruth is pouting with her lip gloss, like behind a veneer of glass.

Agnes (as if in consolation): You know who you remind me of?
Ruth: No, who?
(This is a favorite game that green girls play.)
Agnes: You know who you so are? You are so Catherine Deneuve in *Repulsion*.

And Ruth has heard this before. In fact, she has heard this so many times before that now she finds herself playing Catherine Deneuve, her impenetrability.

Ruth considers the mirror again, hair pulled back with her hand, almost violently.

Ruth: Do you just think I should just cut it off?
Agnes: You mean pull a *Roman Holiday*?
Ruth: I was thinking more Jean Seberg.
Agnes: Yeah, that'd be brilliant.

Ruth looks at her slim neck, pivots and turns. She smiles beneath the pages of a catalogue. Agnes comes next to her. On their knees on the bed they pose for each other in the mirror, two pretty girls.

They compete with each other. Each one wonders whether the other holds more allure in the mirror.

They are tremendously vain. They have fallen madly in love with themselves.

You know, when I first met you, I had a massive crush on you.

Agnes plays peekaboo with herself in the mirror.

You did? Ruth is not surprised. Agnes was always regaling her with stories of her sexual adventures, like the threesome she once had with a tutor from school and his wife. Ruth felt, when Agnes was telling that particular story, that she was trying to test the waters. Which she is trying to do now. But Ruth remains blank and impassive. Opening her eyes wide, feeling the eyelashes tickle her eyebrows.

They watch *Persona* on Agnes's computer. There is no subtlety in this film selection. Agnes loved film. Maybe more than Ruth did. They are in the film of their lives. They are playing themselves. There is a soundtrack always playing. A camera always following them and eyes oh eyes always watching…

What does she want to be? A green girl doesn't like to consider this question. She already is. She is waiting around to be discovered just for being herself.

Ruth falls asleep halfway through. When she awakens she finds Agnes curled around her, her hand stroking the curve of Ruth's stomach, Ruth lets her but doesn't move or make a sound.

The next morning Agnes's red lipstick is smeared all over the sheets.

It would be better if I could only stop thinking. Thoughts are the dullest things. Duller than flesh.

— Jean-Paul Sartre, *Nausea*

Ruth starts using the public toilet on the second floor to avoid the terrible girls. It smells of fart and an older woman's perfume. Escada, Ruth guesses.

Two women hold court in front of the mirrors, addressing themselves through their reflections. They do not turn to the real versions. Girls from an early age learn an uncanny ability to address their mirror image as their identical twin.

How do you like my hair like this?
The brown?
Mmmhmm. It's really an auburn.
It's darker.
Yes.
I think it's quite flattering.
Do you? The woman angles her sagging chin from side to side. She is still dissatisfied.
It matches your skin colour, really nicely.

Ruth locks herself inside a stall. She dries off drops of urine from the bowl, curly swivels of hair, her hair almost touching the pale splatters. She sits down, studies the sign on the door.

To Avoid Loss:
Deposit Handbags on the Shelf

Who does your hair now dear?
Oh I go to a salon in Marylebone.

Ruth repeats this phrase to herself, a salon in Marylebone. Marley-bone. She hadn't a clue where that was. It sounded expensive.

To Avoid Loss. The taste of words. An absurd phrase.

You make me and then you destroy me and you expect me to pick up the pieces again and live. Like I had never met you. It is so easy for you. You are already dead inside.

Nothing comes out. Not even a trickle. Maybe she didn't have to go. Ruth wipes, nonetheless, from front to back, like a good girl.

Outside the two women are still camped out at the mirrors. Ruth washes her hands. She sees herself solemn in the mirror.

The women pause as the stranger approaches. Ruth watches them watching her in the row of mirrors. Her eyes meet the gaze of the woman whose hair is in question. It really was more of an auburn, with little flicks of fire masking wiry grays. Her face harsh in the light. Old lady hair. It ages you, Ruth wants to say, soothingly. She wonders if this is what the friend thinks and does not say.

The woman with the new hair pulls out a plastic hairbrush from her small handbag. She runs it through her severe bob in one neat, unconscious gesture, her face almost sad. In a quiet duet her friend unzips the pocket of her purse, pulling out a lipstick. She focuses closely on coating pinky-brown to her lips.

Ruth lowers her eyes and meditates under the hot rush of the hand dryer.

Ruth wants to escape. She wants to escape outside of herself. Everywhere she goes she wants to confide: Do you know what it's like not to be able to shake your own quality? She doesn't want to be. She doesn't want to live. She wants to lose herself, lose herself in the crowd. She is somehow numbed to the horrors of everyday. Images, other images haunt her brain. The violence of life she observes, blankly. She watches it all unfold. She is not there. A series of shocks and sensations. All along she is trying to figure out life, life, a life which has lost all meaning. Yes, life. Ahh, life. And what about that? Is there nothing else? Life, death, nothing else?

Inside the tube station. The rush hour crush. Ruth is standing exhausted and limp in the queue. Her card won't go through. She is embraced by the arms of the turnstile, like an angry robot mother. A groan behind her. Sorry. She squeaks out. A shamed whisper, a reddening face to an audience of bemused and knowing eyes.

We live in such fear of puncturing the moment, of forgetting our lines.

The car stops in darkness. She is in the corner in the back, pressed against the glass door. The train thick with passengers. Rows and rows. Bodies, bodies, more bodies. Her face grows hot. People pushing her, pressing up against her. She feels herself swaying, swaying. I am going to be sick, she thinks. But she steels herself.

She closes her eyes and tries to die inside.

I am a camera with its shutter open, quite passive, recording, not thinking. Recording the man shaving at the window opposite and the woman in the kimono washing her hair. Some day, all of this will have to be developed, carefully printed, fixed.

— Christopher Isherwood, *Goodbye to Berlin*

Ruth loves the ritual of proper tea. The clink of the cup against the saucer. She feels very English drinking it. After work sometimes or on her days off she goes to her favorite French pastry shop on Greek Street. It has a proper tea service. Today she smiles tentatively at the elderly man with the gray ponytail who noddingly takes her drink order and points her to the table next to the cash register. Sit here, my dear. She is the only customer downstairs. It is the middle of the afternoon.

He recognizes her now and she smiles at him gratefully. Sometimes he makes conversation with her when it is slow. This slightest of recognitions inflames in her a joy that carries her through gray and wettened streets, through cloaks of invisibility.

She opens up the blank notebook she purchased on Charing Cross Road. It is her protective shield. She plans to fill it with all her innermost thoughts and reflections.

She takes pictures in her mind. She stores them away for someday, these images, these experiences, to later document, once she has figured out why she did them in the first place. She watches the world, yet cannot yet articulate her role in it. She cannot fathom the depths. For now she writes dear diary entries in her childish hand dotted by exclamation points. What is it with young women and exclamation points and smiley faces! So afraid of appearing somber, always wanting to appear light and happy and sparkling, even when they are dying inside. Not ever being able to escape the mask that smiles.

She wants to write, really write someday. But she is not fully formed. So she does not write. Not really. Unless attempting to live is a form of attempting to write.

The agony of becoming. This is what she experiences. The young girl. She would like to be someone, anyone else. She wants, vaguely, to be something more than she is. But she does not know what that is, or how one goes about doing such a thing.

A photo shoot is taking place. The old man and Ruth watch silently. A model with long straight brown hair stands outside of the pastry window, wearing an orange flamenco dress. It is freezing outside. The photographer shoots her from inside the café. She is slender and shivering. It seems cruel that a pane of glass separates her and those gorgeously glossy strawberry custard tarts. Ruth's talent is empathy. Her stomach growls. She is hungry. She has only budgeted enough for a pot of tea.

No pastry today? her old man asks. He remembers her sweet tooth.

Not today, she smiles, too wide perhaps, too needy, too grateful.

Lovely, the photographer keeps saying. He is like David Hemmings in *Blow-Up*. Lovely, lovely, lovely.

Delphine: Did he have a camera?
Solange: No.
Delphine: Then how did you know he was an American?

— Catherine Deneuve and Françoise Dorléac in
Jacques Demy's *The Young Girls of Rochefort*

Desire? Desire? Would you like to try?

Ever since the toilet incident Ruth tried to smile without showing teeth. She tried to mime Elspeth's severity. Ever since that day she stopped having lunch with Natalie, who had moved on, swinging her large fake crocodile purse while keeping up with the tall new temp who worked in luggage, as they exited the revolving doors, Natalie bouncing and chattering all the while, like a dot that directs the words to sing, her companion bobbing his head up and down in gentle rhythm. From time to time Ruth caught the boy looking at her as he passed her outside the front entrance. He had red hair, an enflamed face.

Chicago, Illinois. A man points his fingers at her. He had stopped a few paces away, listened for a moment, with head cocked, then walked back. Ruth nods her head. Very good, she replies politely. He bows, the magician revealing his fluttering white dove, his miraculous girl chopped in half, and walks away.

Ruth feels, for a moment, like Audrey Hepburn selling carnations out of a basket. Was her departed land of nativity so inextricably wrapped up in her identity, coiled to her DNA, that it could not be erased, her roots impossible to escape, even across the world, even when she learned to say things exactly as they told her?

Chicago, Hog Butcher for the World, Tool Maker, Stacker of Wheat. The Carl Sandburg poem she recited in school. All the children giggled at the part where she had to say, "They tell me you are wicked, and I believe them, for I have seen your painted women under the gas lamps luring the farm boys."

Chicago, where HE was. Where she could never return. Where she could never escape.

I could not leave you. I was trapped. Perhaps I won't let something go until I've murdered it.

The main visitors to Horrids' illustrious and tacky halls, swinging shopping bags the color of money, riding up and down the Egyptian escalators, were tourists, many of them Americans. The Americans always disappointed to hear a familiar accent. Why, you're American! They would ring with dismay, as if hearing an American voice come out of this seemingly unperturbed blonde was somehow not getting what they paid for.

She would regard them coolly. I know not what thou sayest. Sometimes American customers would be shocked to discover that she was one of theirs, presuming that her soft careful accent was in fact English. But you don't sound American, they'd say.

But you're obviously American, Natalie cried in confusion, when Ruth mentioned this to her. Not all Americans are the same, she insisted, annoyed. Ruth's accent had morphed and changed until it was not quite American and not quite British. Since she had come to London she was now from nowhere. And when she returned (if she ever returned?) she would be from there, not here. Tourist. She was not a tourist. She was something in-between.

Since fragrance was at the front entrance, Ruth often had to play tour guide. She was always hasty to correct. This is the ground floor here, not the first. It's Zed, not Zee. A lift, not an elly-vader. These common errors made her twinge with impatience. Sometimes Ruth remained closed-lipped around Americans, when they asked for directions on the street, clutching their foldout map. Then, she would nod and point, preferring to pass, preferring not to invite the inevitable exchange.

Sometimes older Brits would feign interest in her whereabouts. Where are you from, dear? they would ask. From the States, she would say. If they didn't already know. Oh, that American girl, that American girl. At first they pretended not to understand her and so she was forced to repeat herself, you must speak up, you must annunciate. Which cements your status as child. The perpetual annunciation, my cipher dressed as the Virgin Mary. My stone statue of dove-gray.

She is probed for specifics. Aah, they would say. Chicago. Very cold, is it not? Yes, it is quite cold there, Ruth read from her script. Although most people assumed the United States was one singular group of people. They didn't understand nuances of city and country and north and south and red state or blue state. They didn't get that not all Americans are born-again Christians. They didn't get that America is in the midst of an ideological civil war.

Ruth was on neither side of the war. Yet oh, to be born again. This is what she desires, and every new purchase, every new boy, all of which she imbues with magical properties, a way for her to look at herself anew in the mirror. Like those rebirthing ceremonies in which estranged children, heated pins of violence, are rolled into blankets and the adults sit on the child, simulating a rebirth. That's how Ruth feels. She feels all this pressure, like she is supposed to be born again into this world, and I'm bearing down on her, and nothing is coming out yet. Not even her violence, which she swallows inside. She senses this world infected with godlessness and emptiness and hollowness. She senses the despair. She would like to run down the street naked and screaming, but she can't. It would be terribly impolite and improper.

So she swallows it all. She swallows it all deep deep inside.

Filing into lifts to go to the tube, the squealing sound. Cattle being led to slaughter. Ruth's nervous deer heart beats inside her pale-girl chest. Pushing, Pushing, Pushing. A labor. The lift is a mother-grave spitting out bodies. What if, what if there was a fire or if it got stuck or or...Ruth's mind imagines all sorts of calamities. But still she remains unlined, frozen. The occasional gasp. They are sardines in a can glaring at each other. At this time Ruth resists the urge to yell Fire! Fire! Fire! The evacuation of the scream stored deep inside. The crowded theater of her mind.

The train roars by, shaking her as she stares at her reflection in the steel rumbling past. Doors opening.

Pain has an element of blank;
It cannot recollect
When it began, or if there was
A time when it was not.

It has no future but itself,
Its infinite realms contain
Its past, enlightened to perceive
New periods of pain.

— Emily Dickinson

End of an eternal shift: she is laid out in her tiny bathroom her cheek making love to the linoleum floor. Headache again. Body curled like a paralyzed fetus in a porcelain womb.

The green girl likes to watch herself suffer. My icon of ruin.

Dark sets in, dark and blank and cool. Her body a thing. She steels herself from the crash and roar of the train pain shuttling through her brain. Surrendering herself to the sudden suck of nausea, the swims. From the ceiling she watches herself, watches the floor turn.

Don't move. A whisper. If you move it doesn't hurt as much. She fights down the words circulating around her skull like a bee. A brain tumor probably a brain tumor she has a brain tumor. Thirty days a month a week twenty-four hours. An aneurysm maybe an aneurysm just like her to get an aneurysm.

Shut it out. She shuts the words out, the unrelenting monologue. A whisper. Play dead and they won't hurt you. Play dead. She forces her body to go limp, to make herself go blank inside. More words. A line from somewhere. "Pain has an element of blank."

The words. She is immobile to their force. Around and around in her head. She is dying she will be dead soon. No one will find her for days. The Housekeeping voice the first to break in, dismayed to find a holocaust of dirty towels. They wouldn't know where she came from she kept to herself mostly she was sometimes with that girl with the red hair, the Australian. She would be buried in an unmarked grave for American tourists.

Or.

She would be sent home a solemn casket a symbol of grief. An open casket, perhaps. So young, so lovely. It's Best to Die Young and Leave a Beautiful Corpse. Hopefully tasteful hopefully she wouldn't look too dead or too clownish, like those airbrushed photos at the mall. Whispers at the funeral. So sad So tragic So sudden. And her mother, and her mother, did you hear? Too much loss, she couldn't take it, died from grief. HE would be there, his eyes swelling with tears, tears she never saw fall on real skin. HE would regret that HE had spurned her, a realization too late, that HE had loved her, that HE had always loved her. Stifling a desire to throw himself in after her, an infatuated suitor once more, to follow her underground, into death.

Speaking into the ground a sort of impromptu eulogy:

> *It was mutual, you know.*
> *I wish we had known each other.*
> *I wish I had let myself love you.*
> *A love deferred. Now aborted.*

It would not have been this thing.
It would not have been so terrible.
But then I would have to lose you now.

The words die, fluttering around her like blank strips of paper. All is a hush. The faucet whispers her name in rushing succession, waking her from her morbid obsession. She returns to her body, to the linoleum's cold cruelty, to the banality of her dormitory surroundings. The lowest of moans barely registered amidst all the chaos of outside. It is Friday night. Friday night. Date night. Hate night. The rituals of busied femininity, the elaborate cleaning and preparation of the body. The removal of stray hair of stray thoughts of stray red offenders skirting about on carefully camouflaged faces.

Ruth is not like them. Ruth can still be saved. There is that glimmer in her of something, a sensitivity to this world, maybe too sensitive for this world.

Mind the gap.

That day a group of American girls had exploded through the doors, their laughter ringing. Ruth had recognized them from her floor. She froze, although they tore by without noticing her, scurrying up to the counter stocking French perfumes, with which they proceeded to baptize themselves hysterically. The gaggle of girls. The giggle gaggle. Alone they stare to the ground, their hair hides their eyes—as a group they are protected. The ravishing Spanish girl, a dead ringer for Ava Gardner, attended to them patiently. Ruth your tribe has arrived Elspeth called out. Ruth smirked at her, not thinking of anything clever to say. The smirk was barely noticeable, a slight ripple on her face. The girls around them snickered behind polite hands. Except Ava Gardner, who would never laugh at anybody. She was too kind. Ruth wished they could be friends, except she could never understand anything she said.

Ruth's saliva spools onto the white squares outlined with dirt.

Above all, you must illumine your own soul with its profundities and its shallows, and its vanities and its generosities, and say what your beauty means to you or your plainness, and what is your relation to the ever-changing and turning world of gloves and shoes and stuffs swaying up and down among the faint scents that come through chemists' bottles down arcades of dress material over a floor of pseudo-marble…

— Virginia Woolf, *A Room of One's Own*

Sometimes on her breaks Ruth strolls in and out of the counters of the grandiose hall of the makeup department. Past glistened women desperate for any eye contact, holding jars of miracles. She catches glimpses of herself in the mirrors.

Her eyes feast on the rows and rows of color, like a neatly ordered painter's palette, the pyramid of tubes of lip gloss, gilted compacts bearing a prism of tiny mirrors. Occasionally she would smooth one finger over a glittery palette of eyeshadows with enigmatic names. Types of flora and fauna. Names of movies stars, presidential wives, ordinary girls. Marilyns and Audreys and Sophias and Jackies and Julies and Kathys.

She watches rows of women propped up on chairs, being powdered and glossed and soothingly lied to.

The seductive salesmen with slicked hair and shiny faces preen over them, a flurry of brushes drawn from the tool belts slung around their slim hips.

The frosted lilies working behind the glass counters ignore her when they see that she is not looking to buy.

The tricks are translucent but still you must submit to the ritual.

The eternal question: Would you like to sit down? Do you have time?

They flatter you. They are your friend. You are the sole object of their attention for those minutes. They are like gigolos and confidantes and fairy godmothers all wrapped up into one. They can play straight. They can play gay. They play to your vanity. They worship you. They tell you that you have nice skin. They guess your age much younger than you actually are. You sit greedy for attention, gobbling it up. You are meek, suppliant. You wait patiently as they dab, smooth, pat. You offer up your face to his gaze. He paints on a surprised expression. You look downwards. You look upwards. You are a good girl.

Make me over into someone new, someone who doesn't think such things, someone with memories wiped clean.

Mold me.

You are their raw material. Their Galatea. A fistful of clay, gray, gray, gray, like Ruth's eyes, like the army of everywhere pigeons, like the crisp malice of the autumnal air. If the whole city of London was sliced open all that would come out would be a mess of intestinal gray. (In the world of cosmetics gray is not gray is not gray. There really are countless shades.)

Such lovely lips, eyes, lashes. Such young skin, those brows, that neck. There is always some neglected attribute to draw out, to compliment. You drink it in. It is nourishment you have not received for a while and even if you receive it often you are always thirsty, thirsty for it. To be admired by the vast unknown.

How did you get lured in? You were looking, searching, for something. Something to conceal, to hide, to disguise those flaws, no not the bit of redness there, the shine here, the crow's feet there, the flaws deep inside, the filthy thoughts, the prurient mind. One magical product that would perform all this. You offer yourself up to the counter. No, you need concealers and highlighters and foundations and powders. A product to cancel out the other products.

And finally the reveal. You use the hand mirror they provide. But his adoring eyes have already served as your mirror. Look at you. So lovely, lovely, lovely. The black-clad crowd crowds in for effect, the formerly bored frosted lilies now fawning over the mannequin (that's you!), the slicked-back boys with shiny skin oohing and aahing, clapping their hands with glee.

The girl behind the counter takes over from the male makeup artist. He is an artist. He doesn't handle financial transactions. Earlier, to try to push the expensive makeup brushes on top of the purchase, he said: I am an artist. I must use my tools. You are my canvas. The salesgirl who has played the admiring spectator before now steps in front, clipboard in hand. All cool and business-like. The illusion is gone. They are not your friends. Or, to keep that illusion just a little longer, you know you must buy something. It's part of the exchange, the ritual. She tallies it up. She barters with you still flush with attention. At home is a full makeup bag. But is there a price for seeing oneself anew in the mirror?

This is for the eyes. This is for the lips. This is for the skin. They haggle over the skin.

The skin is necessary of course. You need the skin. Without one of the tricks in the bag it all falls apart. It is a house of cards, your new identity. The makeup artist miraculously reappears to finish the sale. Look at how lovely you look. Your skin looks so young so dewy so glowing. You are reborn. You are luminous. You are lit from within. You flutter under the flattery, docile, obedient.

I'll take it. You say. I'll take it. I'll take the eyes, I'll take the lips, I'll take the skin. I'll take it all.

Wrap up my new face and throw it in a bag.

They give you a face to take home, an actual paper face with colored in instructions. These masks like *memento mori*.

Faces, other faces. I can take mine off and breathe.

The very turmoil of the streets has something repulsive about it—something against which human nature rebels. The hundreds of thousands of all classes and ranks crowding past each other—aren't they all human beings with the same qualities and powers, and with the same interest in being happy? And aren't they obliged, in the end, to seek happiness in the same way, by the same means? And still they crowd by one another as though they had nothing in common, nothing to do with one another, and their only agreement is the tacit one—that each keep to his own side of the pavement, so as not to delay the opposing stream of the crowd—while no man thinks to honor another with so much as a glance. The brutal indifference, the unfeeling isolation of each in his private interest becomes the more repellent and offensive, the more these individuals are crowded together within a limited space.

— Friedrich Engels, quoted in Walter Benjamin's
The Arcades Project

She goes to the same places to avoid getting lost. The perennial return to the center of the beast. She gets out at Tottenham Court Road to a drizzling rain, everyone heading down the stairs in the opposite direction. The Boots, the Sainsbury's, the flower stand. Past the booth of fake designer watches, the table set up of bleeding black signatures—wettening posters of protest, ImpeachTonyBlair DownWithGeorgeBush InternationalTerrorists OutofIraq SendTroopsHome. Ruth shakes her head No not wanting to speak imagining the mere sound of her voice will unleash antagonism, a chorus chant of Crucify her! Crucify her!

She is not political. She is not political yet. She is halting, she is silent, she is unsure. She has not formed any opinions that are her own. Sometimes she hears someone else's opinion, someone more forceful than herself (which is almost anyone) and she says that's good for me too. So malleable she changes identities easily. How else does one figure out who one is? She has flashes of who she could be someday. She speaks in advertising jingles and silly catchphrases and slang. I am not really into politics she would say. She is self-involved. She is volunteering for her own Party of One. The Me Party. Campaigning under the Woe Is Me ticket. My seductive little solipsist. Does she know there is a war going on? Is there a war going on? Turning on the television I thought there was a sale going on, and a season finale, and some celebrities getting a divorce. She knows there is a war waging inside of her. Yet she doesn't know who is winning. She did not vote in the last presidential election. I can't believe it either, but there you are. She is the apathetic youth we always read about. They are silent when not texting away on fancy mobiles or talking on their cell phones about their new game console.

I want to choke these youngsters just to hear them make a sound not banal or repeated or well-behaved. If I choked Ruth she would make a squeaking sound, like a rubber doll. But I won't choke Ruth why would I choke her I love her. If I did choke her it would be in a loving way, like the poster of the Heimlich maneuver you see hung up in school cafeterias and auto shops, the two faceless figures doubled over together in a violent embrace. I would choke her to get at her insides.

Ruth heads down Oxford Street hurriedly, head down, bracing herself against the rain. Jutting in and out of a world of umbrellas an obstacle course. She does not feel like using her cheap Boots umbrella, which might break in the wind. Her nose is forever running. She wipes it on her sleeve, sniffs it back in. I watch her slinking down the street. I see her shoulder blades stick out like a little bird's wings. She is so fragile. Like she is going to blow over. She is sending out signals of distress. These lilting lilies. They shrink from the world. I want to stomp on their fragile stalks not yet formed, those spiky buds creeping up through moist dirt.

The street is decorated with lights for the holidays. The whiff of roasted chestnuts. A blonde man in a black leather jacket matches his stride next to hers. He holds his umbrella over her. The grin of a confident salesman. Can I ask you something? I'm sorry I'm in a hurry. He persists. Who cuts your hair? Ruth feels vaguely humiliated. She knows what this is, a routine to lure her into whatever high street hair salon has paid him to be charming to lonely Americans. But she cannot help smiling at him, shyly shaking her head, saving a fickle strand of wettening blonde hair from falling into her face. He quickens his pace. You'd look absolutely brilliant with something chin-length. I'm not interested, Ruth replies coolly in her feather-voice. No harm to it, he elbows her chummily. She smiles again in spite of herself. Sorry. He stops and as she walks ahead, she looks back at him. He is waiting for her to turn and walk back. He smiles, waves, clipboard in hand. Still waiting. But she turns and keeps on walking.

The end is near! The end is near! Save yourselves! Save yourselves! Her Oxford Circus preacher is prophesizing the rapture from his bullhorn.

She walks in the spaces between the raindrops. She touches her chin to the butt of her cheap Boots umbrella—her face is wet. This kind of rain casts a veil over everything. Somehow one can see more clearly. Old old buildings. People living life somehow.

The question is—does she awake? And what does she awaken to?

I get the impression that her life was one long meditation about nothingness.

— Clarice Lispector, *The Hour of the Star*

She sits in her usual spot by the window at Foyles Cafe. It is still raining outside on soggy red brick. Ruth sits on a stool at the window and watches from up above, dipping her chin into the foam. Umbrellas proceed almost solemnly down the street, rims touching each other almost tenderly. Like schoolchildren proceeding hand in hand.

With the tip of her thumbnail she scratches at the tiny wart hidden under the nail on her second finger. She flicks it meditatively. Her fingernails dirty underneath. She has cuts all over her knuckles. Flick, flick.

She thinks about HIM. How could I have washed off so easily? She wonders.

You leave. You leave and leave.
In the morning, you begin the disentangling. In the morning you go. In the morning you are gone.

She is impressionable. Yet she does not leave an impression. She is like a ghost, a non-thing.

Ruth doesn't know this but a man in the café is watching her too. He has a sketchbook in front of him. He is drawing her outline.

He is sketching her dramatic silhouette. A young girl pensive watching out the window. She is an unknown. He has discovered her. A beautiful sight. She has a beautiful figure, this slip of a girl. He wouldn't mind poking her a bit with his pencil.

The rain has let up momentarily. She gazes at the top level of a double-decker bus stopped outside. The passengers seem unaware that they are being looked at, secure in being so high up from everything. They are in fact naked there, relaxing their tense city selves except for the small dramas of transport, the bumping and pushing and excuse-me's, no pardon-me's. The looking without looking. She catches a boy regarding himself in his reflection, shaking out a light caramel shag, a mustard scarf, a leather jacket the color of toffee. A bled-out brown. She meets his eyes boldly, safe within her bubble. I see you. I see you.

Suddenly Ruth spies the silver-haired shopgirl from Liberty. She seems to be waiting for someone. Her long yet uncertain body against the wall, posing daintily with her paper coffee cup, looking out into the crowds of people with a practiced look that is both cool and yearning. How many sets of eyes warm her. She looks off into the distance. From time to time she looks down at her mobile phone pocketed in her hand. She must be aware of her to-be-looked-at-ness. She is ravishing. She is untouchable. She hangs there like a dress one cannot afford.

She is such a pretty girl. Such a pretty girl. Everyone showers compliments on the pretty girl. She really has a delightful, dreamy quality to her.

That wonderful pouty mouth she has all of her original underclothes. What marvelous coloring. No hairline chips or cracks.

Pushing her way back down the stairs of the tube station, past bodies and briefcases and elbows and legs. Mind your head. Mind your head. Crowds and crowds. She stumbles around, outside of herself, looking at them looking at her.

The train comes shuttling through.

An advert on the train: Feeling knackered? Although Ruth does not know what it means to feel knackered, she has the feeling that this is precisely what she is feeling. The holidays were starting to get to her. The city was starting to get to her. She ached, an indeterminate ache. Her glands were swollen in her throat, under her armpits. She had already called in once that week at work, breathing fragile and penitent at the same time to human resources. If human resources were supposed to be so human, why did they make you feel so alienated? Yes I don't feel well I need to take a personal day. Yes my throat and my head and I'm a bit fatigued you see. She wanted to hibernate, to surrender to the slowness of sick.

She craves her own stand-in, posted politely on her glass window: "The Part of Ruth for the next few days will be played by [fill in the blank]". That's what she needs. She needs her blank to be filled in.

It all began to blur into the same train ride home. Doors closing. Mind the gap. The gap between who she was and who everyone thought her to be. The gap between the past and now, between her fiction and her reality.

The same shift at Horrids. The same bodies. Bodies, bodies, bodies.

Red bodies, yellow bodies, white bodies, brown bodies, black bodies, purple bodies, green bodies, young bodies, old bodies, teenage bodies, middle-aged bodies, girl bodies, boy bodies, androgynous bodies, ambidextrous bodies, muscular bodies, skinny bodies, fat bodies, straight bodies, gay bodies, bi bodies, clean bodies, foul bodies, bodies that smell of smoke, bodies that smell of soap, bodies from the train, bodies from the street, bodies carrying other bodies, bodies in wheelchairs, bodies with strollers, bodies missing appendages, bodies in a hurry, bodies that go slow, bodies that whiz by, bodies that slink past, bodies that talk, bodies that are mute, bodies that don't exist, bodies with shopping bags, bodies with large leather purses, damp bodies, dry bodies, bodies with the coldest of hands, bodies with the softest of skin, bodies with bored faces, bodies with scarred faces, bodies with no faces, bodies chewing bubble gum, bodies eating crisps, bodies on phones, bodies with umbrellas, bodies with other bodies, art bodies, business bodies, celebrity bodies, nobodies, mommy bodies, daddy bodies, brother bodies, sister bodies, bodies with bellies, bodies with breasts, hunched-over bodies, rich bodies, poor bodies, bodies who have never worked a day in their life, nice bodies, mean bodies, strange bodies, familiar bodies, British bodies, American bodies, bodies who say cheers, bodies who say thanks, bodies who ignore you, bodies who say *bonjour*, bodies of all nations, bodies wearing turbans, bodies whose skirts touch the floor, bodies all bundled up, bodies too naked, bodies with beards, bodies with long hair, bodies that tap by on heels, bodies that shuffle by, bodies bodies bodies…

To all of these she proffers her Desire.

I have a part of you with me. You put your disease in me. It helps me. It makes me strong.

— Isabella Rossellini in David Lynch's *Blue Velvet*

Agnes and Ruth are at a pub on the East End. Agnes is wearing a red-and-black checkered long-sleeved minidress. Red heels. Her hair now in glossy dark brown curls. Her makeup done up like Isabella Rossellini in *Blue Velvet*. A blur of red lips. Eyelids bedded in deep blue. Like a bruised angel. She occupies herself tonight by twirling around on her barstool, sipping her red wine. Ruth watches her twirl, sip, twirl, sip, twirl, twirl. Her stockings are ripped. There is a pale moon on her knee. She cultivates a more mysterious air as a brunette. As a redhead everything was shock and fright.

Do you ever get the feeling a camera is following you around at all times? She brings her face up close to Ruth. Her teeth are stained gray from the wine. Yeah, I think so. Yeah, me too. Agnes's voice is dreamy. Ruth feels like she is just there in order to speak the supporting role, a character in Agnes's play. Agnes digs into her purse, finds her silver cigarette case and holder. She lights up, breathing out billows of smoke with each turn. Ruth can't help admiring her. You should have been an actress, she says. What? I said, you should act. On stage or something. I hear that sometimes. She warms up to this her favorite subject. What if life were like that Peter Greenaway film, and every room I walk into the color of my outfit changes, like Helen Mirren's.

Agnes is now looking around the room, looking for something, someone, something else. Ruth doesn't know what she is looking for, but the room disappoints her tonight. Oh, Ruth. Agnes finally says. I'm so bored, I'm so terribly, terribly bored. She waves her empty glass at the bartender at the other end of the bar.

Another red wine? Yes, could you, please? She oozes flirtatiousness.

Care for another? The bartender leans in with his arms folded across the bar, and taps his fingers against Ruth's glass. A vodka and cranberry. Her voice comes out little girl. She liked the dark pink of vodka and cranberries. Nod. Coming up. His accent is thick, Scottish. As he makes her drink—cocking his head from time to time to take an order—Ruth studies him. Agnes has sprung down from her stool to accost a boy she knows from across the room with a spiky hairstyle called the Hoxton hawk. How do I look she fixates on Ruth's face as if Ruth's eyes were her mirror. Fine fine. Agnes's nose wrinkles with displeasure. Fine just fine? You look lovely, Ruth soothes. Lovely lovely lovely.

Ruth is now alone at the bar. This is why I don't like going out with Agnes, she thinks. The trains stop running at a certain time. If she abandons her tonight she doesn't know what she will do. She doesn't have enough money for a cab, and she doesn't know where to find a cashpoint. She hasn't figured out how to take the bus yet. To Ruth the circuitous rituals and routes of London bus transit are transportational enigmas she knew she could never brave alone.

When the bartender returns with her pink drink she smiles at him. How much? He waves his hand, bringing it down to barely rest on her wrist, which he strokes once with one finger. She stares back, mimicking his boldness.

Smug face, smug eyes, smug lips. He had a slight bruise around one eye, that lent him a sort of dangerous vulnerability. A bit of a brute.

There are strangers who wear your face.

You remind me of someone.
And who's that? Smirk.
Just someone…she trails off.
Another smirk, twisting his towel into the wet glass. Oh, yeah?

He leaves again. He returns. Ruth feels a sort of fatality about everything. Listen, he hesitates for a moment. A slow smile. I'm going to take my break now in back. Would you care to accompany me? Ruth shrugs. A heart thump, a start of panic.

Almost in slow motion he takes her hand and leads her behind the bar and out to the back room. There are coats sprawled everywhere like deflated corpses. We can go downstairs. It's more private, he says. Ruth nods. She is on mute. She follows him down the gray concrete stairs, tentative, not wanting to trip.

They are in what appears to be a supply room. It is just the two of them. Ruth shivers. He could rape her right now, she knows. She has gone to a strange place with a strange man, and she is drunk. She has agreed to meet him in the equivalent of a dark alley. And here she is. That is how Ruth approached so much of her life—and here she is. She finds herself in situations. She could leave. She couldn't leave. She wouldn't know how to leave. She is frozen to the spot. She is also curious to see what is going to happen in this film of her life. Will it be a horror film? This is certainly not shaping up to be a romance picture. It is a cautionary tale. It is at least R-rated. R for rape not romance. R for ruin. R for run, Ruth, run. But Ruth won't run. She doesn't hold the strings. She is the unwilling puppet. She is not the author of the Book of Ruth.

She is curious to see what will happen, a gaper's block of self. She is the voyeur of herself. She is willing, a willing victim. If not wanting then willing although she is wanting she has a hole a void and perhaps he has what she needs to fill it.

The boy sits down on a keg. Pats his legs like a department-store Santa. As if on cue Ruth lowers herself onto his lap. He nuzzles her neck. He paws at the hot triangle underneath her skirt. He inches his hand down her pantyhose, fingering her. He plays with her like this for a while. She lets him even though it hurts and she would rather be at home, in her room, reading fashion magazines. She is still, like a doll, only occasionally writhing about in discomfort.

Finally he takes his finger out. He licks it. This is supposed to be sexy. Mmmhmm, she purrs as if on cue. I don't even know your name darling. Ruth hesitates. It's Jessica, she says. That's the name of her favorite model. Hi Jessica, I'm Alistair. Hi, she whispers. He kisses her mouth. His chin, patched with black wire, scratches her face. She kisses him back, tentatively at first, then with her mouth open wide, twisting around on his lap.

You smell nice.
It's Desire, she breathes.

She traces the purple bruise around his eye. Did it hurt? she asks. His eyes flicker mockingly.

She puts her hand on the crotch of his jeans, warm and sweaty. He moans. The vodka-and-cranberries has made her feel all loose and wavy, unsure of herself. Leaning over, she kisses him. Her tongue licking him like a cat, her blonde hair hanging in her face.

She conjures up Deneuve in *Belle de Jour*. She allows filthy paws on her pristine body.

She has fucked and fucked until there is nothing left of her. How many of the unworthy has she let into her body? She has lost count. This is her "experiment." She is "experimenting." Sex is just something else she lets inside of her, like images from TV. She lets anyone, anything inside, to ignore the gnaw of loneliness, which comes anyway.

Does she mourn her young body riddled with violations? She does not know what to mourn.

Of all the terrible things that I have let inside of my body, you are King Terrible.

He stands her up, lifts her skirt up above her waist. He kisses her stomach, nuzzling her through her underwear, his wiry chin poking through. He undresses her like a child.

(This role really calls for nudity. It helps you understand the character more.)

He stands there and looks at her, every porcelain inch of her, a curious expression on his face. To see herself as desirable in their eyes. That is the trade. She presses her breasts against his chest, his crotch. She twitches her tail. She is seductress. She has learned how to be sexy from the covers of men's magazines.

All I can do is look at her breasts. She has perfect French breasts. They are pert and taut with brownish-pink nipples. I want to stroke them. I am in awe of these lovely breasts—not like mine at all, maternal and massive and saggy.

He strokes her head, he presses it down. She obeys. She kneels down on the cold stone floor with an almost devoutness. On her knees she bows forth unzips his jeans takes his penis with its taste of urine in her mouth and pretends to ravish it. She pretends she is one of the women advertised in the phone booths. This is a part she is playing. It is the part of herself, her self who is not herself. He strokes her head more, tucking her hair behind her ears, almost a gesture of love. She sucks and tugs for a while, then takes it out of her mouth, looking at him. She is a bit bored and her mouth is sore. And her lip gloss feels coated across her cheeks. She wonders if he will give her money for a cab ride home.

She watches him strip off his T-shirt, throw his pack of smokes on the floor, pull off his boots and his jeans. His body covered in a dark fur. She has seen it all before, as if in a dream. But she is not really there. Not really there. She retreats inside her bubble.

She deadens herself. This self, this self not yet formed. What damaging effect can that have, that ability to vacate the premises?

With a moan, he lies down on top of her.

It is as if they had destroyed beforehand the words with which one might grasp them.

— Rainer Maria Rilke, *The Notebooks of Malte Laurids Brigge*

Ruth grits her teeth at the tourists who cannot read the Please Stand On Your Right sign posted above the escalator. It is morning rush hour. She is late. Again. She has overslept. Again. Is she conscious of these tiny insurrections of the self? Her train roars past downstairs.

Excuse me! Excuse me! She pipes up to the crowd of Germans in front of her, cameras swinging like oversized medallions. They either don't hear or don't understand or don't care. She grows more and more furious with every plea. But the Excuse me! comes out the same, high-pitched, fluttering, lost in the air. She does not push herself down the escalator, like she has seen Londoners do.

She misses the whish of the doors of the next train. Business suits dive inside like clowns. A briefcase, hand, tie, knee almost get caught in the door. Ruth gasps. She waits for the next train, the next train, the next, the next. All full.

Finally she catches one that is almost completely empty, like a phantom train. Except for two men in long robes across from her. They are praying hunched over a book. The one with the olive skullcap has muddy sneakers with laces pricked up like elephant ears. The one with the black skullcap bends over his shiny wingtips.

She looks out the window and sees herself reflected in the darkness. She automatically smiles at herself.

Late for work. Again. The terrible girls roll their eyes at each other as she races in, having sprinted from the tube stop, cheeks flushed, head down, muttering inarticulate apologies.

She rushes downstairs towards the locker room. Where's the fire? Slow down. She can't. She is always late, late, late. She must pass by the luggage department to go to the locker room. He is behind the desk, leaning back, like he has nothing to do. The boy with the enflamed face. He waves at her as she passes, a lightning bolt, as if he had been expecting her. She waves back.

Once she has stored her belongings in her locker (she just throws them in there, she has forgotten the combination on her lock), she approaches him. She points at herself by way of introduction. Ruth. His red head bobs up and down gently. Rhys. Rhys that's a nice name where is that from. I'm from Wales. Wow. She says. She doesn't know why she says that. She doesn't really know where Wales is. She thinks it's near Scotland. You're a temp right? Rhys asks. That's right. Me too.

Just then the horrible head strolls past them, as if he had been looking for her. His thick leather face frowns.

Well, I'm being beckoned. Sorry. (Why is she always apologizing?) For some reason Ruth feels compelled to hold out her hand. He holds out his long bony hand and they shake. He is freckled all over, little brown spots confusing each other. Nice to meet you, Rhys, was it? A pleasure, Ruth. As if he already knew her name.

And then afterwards, all day, she takes with her a tiny flame of something, what it is, she does not know.

Rush hour. Heading home. Car so crowded everyone crushes up against each other. Smell of spearmint gum, beer, sweat, hairspray, warming chicken breasts collapsing in a plastic Sainsbury's bag. A man is behind Ruth the entire ride home. He presses up against her. We are partners for the ride she thinks. I allow him to press up against me, to make room. It is almost curiously moving.

I'm afraid of everything—birds, storms, lifts, needles—and now, this great fear of death...

— Corinne Marchand in Agnès Varda's *Cléo from 5 to 7*

She has all of these questions she carries around with her she doesn't know whom to ask. They are the questions of a child. Sometimes at night she sits up and thinks of these whys, like they are filling a page.

Why do people leave? Why are we here? What happens when we die? This is what she really wanted to know.

Where was her mother? Everyone fed her metaphors and lies. All the answers were excuses. She is with us now. Literally? No, not literally. She needed to know answers. Was her mother there? Actually watching after her? She needed to know.

How come when people talk of death or dying, they look up? she wonders. Like they're hoping to find the belly of some traveling hotel? She thinks that perhaps people need to visualize something. It eases them to imagine heaven as a sort of extended holiday. She is beginning to think that people tell themselves fantasies.

But what is the alternative? she wonders. We are born, then we die. Nothing else? Nothing, nothing else?

Sometimes she needed to shudder out loud at night, a quick lunge of air, in recognition of her own mortality.

What do you think happens afterwards? she asks Agnes, who is dyeing her hair back to an orangey-red. The rickety white sink in her room had become permanently dyed with the black and red splotches of an abstract painting. Ruth is sitting on Agnes's bed, smoking out the window. Smoking was something to do. Every time she struck a match she could imagine that first cell of terror forming until it grew and grew and became her. And still she kept smoking, filling up her chest until it felt tight.

What do you mean afterwards?
You know, when we die.

Ruth strokes her prickly hairs on her leg, studying her messy shaving patterns, running her hand over mysterious bruises.

Oh I don't know. Agnes has wrapped her hair in a towel and is now plucking her eyebrows.

How could you not think about it? What else is there to think about? Agnes shrugs.

Later they sit in bed and watch *Stage Door* on Agnes's laptop. The boarding house of actresses remind them of their Hell, complete with terrible food, although the girls skirting the halls in their bathrobes are not imbued with the *bon mots* of Ginger Rogers and Katharine Hepburn, in the roles of warring roommates.

Hepburn: I see that in addition to your other charms you have that insolence generated by an inferior upbringing.

Rogers: Fancy clothes, fancy language, and everything!
Hepburn: Unfortunately, I learned to speak English correctly.
Rogers: That won't be much use to you here. We all talk Pig Latin.

(Afterwards)

Agnes (yawning): Aren't you sick of this place? It's such rubbish. I feel like I'm going to die here.
Ruth (looking about at the green walls closing in): It's pretty terrible.
Agnes: I can't believe we have a curfew. Or that we can't let men into our rooms. It's like we're still in Victorian times.
Ruth: I can't believe we have to turn in our keys when we leave. It's like we're living in a hotel.
Agnes: A hotel. A hotel! An institution with towel service! The women's ward of Bedlam! (throwing herself on the bed with theatrics that would have made Hepburn proud).

So in December, Ruth moved with an insistent Agnes to the East End, into a shivering attic flat on Brick Lane above a curry restaurant. There was one large room in which they both slept, Agnes in the bed and Ruth on a mattress on the floor, a creaky bathroom with the sad absence of both a bathtub and hot water, and then a kitchen off to the side. Out of the kitchen window Ruth could watch men in shawls walk with canes down the cobbled street or stand outside their fruit stands and video stores, conversing with the evening rush. Bengali men stood outside the neon signs to beckon people into their restaurant, bartering over Londoners who had arrived already loud and inebriated in black minicabs. Ruth referred to them as the callers. Sometimes as Ruth walked home from work, a caller would keep pace with her, as she repeatedly shook her head no. No, she was not interested in having a lovely dinner tonight. No, she didn't care if it was half-off. They were worse than the flierers in their persistence.

Many evenings Ruth had the flat to herself. Agnes usually out, somewhere. Sometimes Agnes would not come home until the next morning, when she would then try to interest Ruth in her stories of her snogging and shagging, which Ruth thought should be sounds zoo animals made.

In the evening when she would get home from work she sat on a stool by the windows and watched the goings-on like a film unfolding. Relaxing into the stoic pose of the observer. She would smoke and watch the world go by. She smoked because she craved something to do with her hands, that delicate interplay of light and cup and first inhale. Craved the repetition of it. It was so difficult sometimes to be still in a room, alone with oneself. To bare oneself to the lonely.

I was never anything to you, was I? Nothing, nothing at all.

On Friday and Saturday nights sometimes fights would break out among the inebriated, and from her privileged distance she would watch the violent pantomime, their silver-haired landlord talking to the bobbies when they eventually arrived. Sometimes people would glance up and see her watching them. She appeared to be quite deep in thought, but actually she wasn't thinking of much at all.

Sometimes her mind was completely vacant. Sometimes no one was at home. The only thing she could mourn was herself.

40 percent off, 50 percent off, Half Off Half Off.
40 percent, 50 percent, Half Off, Half Off, Half Off for you nice ladies tonight…

To live is to feel oneself lost.

— José Ortega y Gasset

Agnes always wanted to go out. Out was better than in. In was inside, in was interior, in was introspection. Outgoing was much more preferable.

Usually they met up in central London, near Agnes's work, teeming with rabble-rousers standing outside pubs beer in hand pouring down cobblestones occupying bored queues at cashpoints. Or they went to dark places in their new neighborhood, a complex web of alleys and streets Ruth had not yet tried to learn. Agnes could never understand why Ruth refused to go back to that pub with the bartender. That was the scene in which to be seen. You are terribly BIZ-arre Ruth, she would whine, but Ruth remained intractable.

Agnes needed to wash away the grind, the coffee grinds and molesting eyes of the masses (she preferred the molesting eyes of the select chosen few). Drinking was the best way to wash away CoffeegirlAgnes, who was different than AgnesAgnes. CoffegirlAgnes wore a different costume, it was a mandated uniform, which is such an insult to Agnes because Agnes is an individual. Ruth was the ear to Agnes's steady stream of complaints as they pounded down the cobblestones.

It was starting to be cold outside at night. Cold and gray, always gray. Ruth sometimes needed the realization of her embodied air, that blow of frigid smoke, to remember that she was still breathing. Ruth kept her right hand in her pocket, since she had lost her glove, gloves that she had bought at Horrids with her discount, nice inky cashmere gloves. She picked at the little wart in her pocket, clicking her nails together. It made her upset to even think about that lost glove hiding in some dark alley, cold and alone, without its twin. Agnes wore a vintage orange belted coat that exactly matched her hair, with a shaggy cream fur collar and identical shaggy fur earmuffs, her hands hanging raw and pink. Black chipped nail polish.

They sit and wait. They warm the backs of bar stools. What are they waiting around for? They are waiting around to be discovered. In the meantime they order drinks or have drinks bought for them. They start getting drunk. If she drank too much then Ruth would wake up and the only pain she felt would be the indeterminate pang to her head, comforting in its constancy, evicting all other thoughts that dared to enter except the banal necessities of the present. And when Ruth drinks then Ruth can be brave can escape outside of herself.

They put on a show. The show that green girls know so well. Posing for the invisible eye. They wait for their photos still wet touch don't touch Ruth is laughing in every frame drunk drunkener than drunk drunk Agnes is serious poised she knows how to pose for her picture she knows her good side.

They are at a karaoke bar. Agnes has dragged a limp Ruth onstage. Agnes wants them to sing Madonna's "Like a Virgin." (Right.)

As Agnes writhes about on stage, on her knees, Ruth stands in the back and giggles, swinging back and forth, back and forth, a drunken metronome. Agnes is front and center and Ruth is off in the corner she is just laughing laughing laughing her throat open, head thrown back she is laughing so much she can't stop she can't stop stop stop. (But later lying in bed that's not how it works out. Ruth is the star moaning into the microphone she is the seductive kitten and HE is standing in the back, behind the crowd, watching her. HE only has eyes for her.)

They are at a club on the East End. The sweaty masses. Agnes has on her fetish-gear, purchased at one of the sex shops in Soho. She is Charlotte Rampling in *The Night Porter*. Ruth wears a blue wig. She teeters around on knee-high stripper boots purchased on the high street. Eyes lined extra thickly for protection. They sneak out to the bathroom and insert a magical powder of bravery up their nose. Ruth can now be SexxxyRuth. The world's just the two of them. They are on display and everyone else is watching. They are dancing what they think is erotically. Men are watching so it must be working. They strike poses. They are cock teases. They press themselves against each other. At this moment there is no one Ruth loved more than Agnes, and no one Agnes loved more than Ruth, they were the same, they were two for one, a package deal. They purr and writhe. The camera snaps. They sloppy girl-kiss for the finale. They are lesbians just for the night.

Sometimes Agnes gets lucky lucky with someone else someone who can better fill her void and then she abandons Ruth a cast-off lover. This is the goal, isn't it? Ruth is supposed to be happy for her but usually she's just annoyed. If they are near their neighborhood

Ruth has to walk, head bent down, arms crossed, praying with each step that no one jumps out from the shadows. If in central London she takes the train home alone, heart beating around the darkness of Soho until she finds her way to the mainland of Oxford Street, emptied of its daily inhabitants, their ghosts twirling around litter of Coke cans and yesterday's headlines on the abandoned street.

And the next day her gigantic dark glasses must shield her from the world's harsh reality. She stumbles through the city, dry and shaky. It is too much outside. The studies and the stares. Pale underneath her sunglasses. Reflecting the masses of people outside, the feeding frenzy. Her protective lenses. Her protective film she wears over herself. My actress and her protective film. Her careful body of lace edges.

Who am I? If this once I were to rely on a proverb, then perhaps everything would amount to knowing whom I "haunt".

— André Breton, *Nadja*

Liverpool Street Station was like a giant cathedral devoted to those in transit, filled with light and masses of travelers. Everyone had somewhere they needed to go. A crowd gathers before the rail schedules, eyes pointing up at the flickering times. Gazing up at the heavens of when and where.

Ruth loved the fruit man at the station, who set up shop just outside the metal arms of the exit. Straight out of *Mary Poppins.* He was white-haired, wizened. She buys grapes from him. Three quid, miss. He shakingly places the grapes in a white paper bag, which he holds in his mouth as he holds out his palm to collect the steady drop of three pound coins. Sometimes other people worked that stand, like the man in the lumberjack shirt, and then Ruth would miss the old man's gentle spasms.

She now has a long distance to walk from the train station to her flat, but she measures out each step of her journey. Sometimes she smokes a cigarette, to keep time, for something to do, the cold pink hand in one pocket. She rounds the corner to the dark stretch that led to Spitalfields market. She eats the grapes unwashed while walking home.

The Spitalfields church looms through the distance with its gray outline. Like a ghost that jumped out of the corner.

I haunt your haunts. You hide in dark corners while I pass.

Can you please spare 40p? A wild-eyed scarecrow of a man, dressed in rags, storms at her from the opposite direction. Ruth shakes her head, and veers out of his path. He sputters in disgust and charges up to someone else. Again, futile. He throws his hands up in the air and walks away, with wide paces. He always demanded the same amount. The please was always choked out with a sort of vitriolic frustration. He had a curious approach, a strangely aggressive tactic, one of purposeful antagonism, terrorizing the inhabitants of the street. He had a frustrated air of defeat even before asking. He didn't even try to be polite. Why should I give you money? she once heard a woman snap back at him. He stomped away, glaring.

Ruth wonders to herself what exactly 40p would get 40p man. She had seen him on more than one occasion head into the bookie's next to Tesco's, so perhaps this is what kept him roaming up and down that same dark corridor, some sort of beggar's purgatory. 40p man was the first real obstacle on her walk home.

Once she successfully scurried past him, head down, walking fast in the dark, anxious not to make eye contact, there were two other beggars that dotted the stretch past the market. They were part of the chain gang holding up copies of their charity rag. They approached you with the devoutness and humility of dirt-smudged saints, posed in various positions of submission, like a homeless *commedia dell'arte*. 40p man appeared to be their leader. She sometimes saw the trio of forgotten men heading to the corner newsagent on Old Street. Trading their money in for cigarettes.

Past the market, closed in the evenings, there were two pubs on Commercial Street filled with nine-to-fivers. On more moderate days they would be outside clutching their pint glasses of amber-colored liquid. On Commercial and Hanbury she would sometimes have to shuffle by thick throngs of Jack the Ripper tours congregating at stops where prostitutes met their death. Whenever Ruth thought about those prostitutes she had to hold her belly, imagining the burn of it being slashed. Then a thrill, a shiver, almost of delight. Once she turned on the cobblestones of Hanbury and walked past the vintage shop that had hundreds of high-heeled shoes hanging in its windows—sky blue and canary yellow and lipstick red—she then had to deal with the parade of those heading to the curry houses, especially on weekends, and the callers luring them.

A skinny teenager with a gelled flat-top, who stood outside of her landlord's restaurant on the intersection of Brick Lane, took particular delight in harassing her. He yelled out to her as he saw her coming. C'mon, let me see your beautiful smile. When the older callers were there they would say something to him that would make him stop. But tonight no one is there, it is still too early. Ruth tries her best to look invisible, a timid smile plastered on her face, eyes downcast, hurrying hurrying past. She scavenges for her keys in her purse. This time her torturer keeps pace with her and stands between her and the doors, leaning on the painted white door dirtied with scuffmarks. The shiny-haired sadist couldn't have been more than 17. His lids only half-open. Agnes had told her that many of the younger callers, a gang of boys who lived in council housing nearby, were heroin addicts. Now this one's zeroing in on our heroine. Need some help with the bags, pretty lady? Ruth eyes him as meanly as she can. Excuse me, she warbles. Grinning, he moves aside so that she can pass, although he momentarily stands in the doorway, almost as if to prove that he can. All right, all right, I was just trying to be friendly. I was just trying to be friendly. That's what they all say. The feign of innocence. The pretense of Samaritan impulses. In her mind she spits in his face. She spits in all of the faces of the strange men on city streets who torture her with their stares. But on her face is that same, slight smile.

She walks upstairs in complete darkness, past the moan of her downstairs neighbors, a Spanish couple always going at it. The light bulb in the staircase has been out for weeks. No one has said anything to the landlord. Her creaking footsteps echo. No one's home. She sits in the kitchen with its broken tiled floors, its windows creaking against the wind, and lights a candle, playing with the wax, feeling the warmth stiffen on her hands. There's no one home. HOME. A meditation, a myth. She has forgotten what home ever was.

Her stomach cramps and rebels. Nausea. Ruth hurries to the toilet and surrenders to a quick sick. Groan. Knives. It is that time. Again. The red mixes in with the brown, a filthy paint.

The toilet will not flush. She pushes on the silver lever, up and down, up and down, a performance of futility. She sees her pale reflection in the silver, hovering, hovering over herself.

One cannot long remain so absorbed in contemplation of emptiness without being increasingly attracted to it. In vain one bestows on it the name of infinity; this does not change its nature. When one feels such pleasure in non-existence, one's inclination can be completely satisfied only by completely ceasing to exist.

— Émile Durkheim

On her day off she decides to get her nails done. The Horrids holiday party was coming up, and the temporaries were invited. This is now occupying her thoughts. She wanders into a place in Covent Garden past the billboard for *The Lion King*, the musical, past the cobblestoned street of cobblers kebobs fishandchip shops, near mannequins posed and doubled over in the windows of Zara's and Marks and Spencer's.

Pick a color. A casual order. Her choices are a garish pageant of metallic purples or reds, then a parade of Easter pastels. She thinks about asking for "Tiger Red" because she just saw *The Women*, but only Agnes would understand that joke. She can't decide in time so settles on an innocuous enough clear varnish.

I'll just take this.

The girl looks at her puzzled. A gold chain dangles in between her deeply tanned breasts. She is already cotton swabbing cold on each of Ruth's fingers. Ruth's nose pricks with nostril-flaring chemicals.

Ruth remembers accompanying her mother to the salon as a little girl, a warm place where she could run around slipping on wet curls blanketing the floor, her mother waving under a hot-air helmet. The feel of her gold wedding ring, a comforting heaviness, when she held Ruth's hand, careful not to smudge her nails freshly painted coral, which Ruth would stare at transfixed. Sometimes the manicurists painted Ruth's and her sister's little nails, hard squares of chewing gum. Ruth always wanted the shiniest. Hot pink covered in rainbow glitter.

No color? The girl looks curiously at Ruth.

No. Just clear.

The girl shrugs.

There were certain ritualized movements Ruth was expected to perform when accepting a manicure that she did not know, or always forgot, planting her hand in a clear bowl of lukewarm soapy liquid post-file, tickling the stones at the bottom, holding out her hand for the obligatory up-to-the-elbow massage with a cheap peach-scented lotion, her arm instead flopping like a fish back down to the dishtowel-covered table. Her hand arches a scared cat's back as opposed to calmed flat, a willing accomplice. Relax, the girl scowls. She kneads Ruth's arm angrily, pulling at her knuckles with a smack.

They both keep eyes glued to the monitor overhead blaring music videos. An anonymous boy band, grunting and posturing. Followed by an anonymous girl band, grunting and posturing. Then the libidinal cooing of the singer whose perfume Ruth pushes onto the masses.

Ruth wonders what it would be like to be a manicurist. She thinks about it and can only conjure up Deneuve in *Repulsion*. Or the girl in that Godard film who is doing the nails of Juliette who is a prostitute, and turns out to be one as well. Then that scene in which the two of them walk around naked with Pan-Am bags on their heads.

All right—expert shake and twist of one last bottle, brushing on the final coat of wet. Fifteen minutes to dry. The girl gets up and leaves, snapping her gum one final time.

Ruth sits alone at the table, fingers fanned out, staring at her hands.

Afterwards she wanders around the high streets to look at dresses. A desperate, heated search. But what she is searching for is something elusive. Changing room of Topshop. Cowboy boots fitted over tight jeans walk past. She hears the meaningful clink of bangles. The swish of skirts worn by girls dressed as gypsies. Ruth stands in the changing room, in her bra and cotton underwear from Marks and Spencer. She surveys herself. She turns to the side and studies herself in profile.

Oh, how much it takes to groom oneself for a party she thinks. There are the nails, and then perhaps she should get waxed, her upper lip feels furry, it yearns for that brightening strip of pain. And then she would like to get stockings, gold, silky stockings they sell at Horrids. She didn't know why she was worried about it. It was a week away. But she would almost rather not go. It was too much effort. To look passable. To look pretty enough. To make sure all the seams lined up and everything matched and she looked as much the her in her mind's eye as she possibly could. She did not know even who she was dressing up for. So much effort to go through to smile smugly at her mirror reflection. Saying, yes, this is you on your best day.

She puts her clothes back on, and leaves, depositing her dresses in the arms of the attendant.

Outside, a cold slap of freeze. She hears her preacher in the distance, bellowing into his bullhorn:

A life devoted to things is a dead life, a stump.

The eternity of the tube. Pushing down steps thick with bodies, a cattle cavalcade. On the train home: businessmen, emitting beer from their mouths, stench from their armpits, reaching in, holding onto the bars, pressing up against her.

Is this a wind-up? she overhears.
Are you winding me up?

Ruth imagines her fellow passengers crushing tightly wrapped young bodies with that drunken force. Come on baby, just a little more, come on baby, dearie, love.

Blondes make the best victims. They're like virgin snow that shows up the bloody footprints.

— Alfred Hitchcock

The camera skirts around the fragrance department, like the device Hitchcock used in *Rope*. Colored perfume bottles on mirrored trays like little glass houses. Mirrors everywhere. A maze of thickly made-up faces. Mannequins behind glass. Full pouts. Distant expressions. They seem more alive than the people inside. A woman applies lipstick while crouched behind the counter. Another hunches below the till to eat. Another sends a text furtively hands tucked inside her apron.

A roomful of robotic smiles, parroted pleasure. A roomful of automated transfers. There is a glitch in the machinery. One shopgirl asks the customer twice if she wants her receipt in the bag. She has been standing on her feet all day. She is exhausted. The customer, politely, says yes both times. Sometimes there is an attempt at contact. The false compliment on either side of the counter. Nice necklace. Nice eyeshadow. Nice cage you got there. The bubbles of niceness float up, but they are not real feelings. Perhaps people go to a department store to cool the ache of loneliness lingering in their belly. To release the hysteria bubbling up in one's throat. So lonely, so longing for any interaction.

A close-up on Ruth, my Hitchcock blonde. Who is the girl behind the counter? I wish to know her. I want to say to her: It must be terrible to be stuck here. I want to look deep into her eyes and say: I see you. You are not invisible to me. I see you. But the girl will smile blankly. Would you like me to pop your receipt in the bag? As if someone had pulled her string. I am just a moment in her day. I am a blip on her screen. Next please next please until it was over and her shift was done and she could die and be reborn. She only exists from the waist up. She is my girl miraculously sawed in half. This was the only world she knew that day. The world behind the counter.

Does she cry out to be saved?

In the East End, hurrying home after closing at Horrids, lowering her head, her shoulder blades going in. Shielding herself from wind and stares. A stream of blankness. She spies the shadow of a young woman appearing in the distance walking towards Ruth, towards Liverpool Street Station. With a jolt, she realizes it is Elspeth. Then she remembers Olly mentioning something about playing with his jazz group nearby. At first Ruth feels violated. Elspeth, in her neighborhood. But she looks almost lovely, walking alone, head down, arms crossed, black sleeve on black. Like the Virgin Mary, Ruth thinks. As their paths cross Elspeth lifts her head almost as if she had been expecting her and smiles brightly. Not a word is spoken. And then Ruth feels almost tender towards this pale aloof girl, so in love with a boy as to go out at night to follow him and then walk home alone. This is her world more than mine, she thinks. In this city, this London, she is merely only a visitor, a tourist and not a tourist, somewhere in between. She can leave any time. She would leave. And maybe Elspeth would never leave her solitary circle, her train ride there, her walk home here, her trips out at night. This is the globe she was born inside, with its little white shaky pieces settling over a toy city, that you turn over and say Ahh…

The two girls are at home, making up their faces as if they were the Sistine Chapel. Silently inventing themselves. Agnes had invited herself as Ruth's plus-one to the Horrids holiday party. Ruth is kneeling on their floor in front of the mirror, carefully making up her face. Agnes had let her borrow her green sparkly eyeshadow. Ruth fingerpaints it on her lids, it sticks on the tips of her fingers and under her nails like green tinsel. She keeps on fucking up the black liquid cat's eye, so she traces the swoop thicker and thicker. She studies the angry red zit on her cheek, considers coloring it in as a beauty mark (Agnes says no) so she dots concealer on it with a semi-clean finger. She is wearing the same black work dress she wears almost every day (she flapped her arms through a mist of perfume to mask her B.O.), but she's added her new stockings and a pair of Agnes's gold door-knockers. Agnes is wearing a red dress, red stockings, red shoes, red hair flipped up. She is twirling on her fifth coat of lipstick, blotting on an old copy of a *Metro* that she then throws back on the floor. Their flat was already filthy. These girls lived like pigs. Walking on their red carpet of dirty clothes that they picked up from the floor, sniffed and wore. They had more important things to do. They must groom themselves, they do not have time to clean.

They have to get ready for their audience, for the flash and wave. To Agnes there was always this Everyone appraising them at all times. And maybe there was. The world is always the audience for young girls, and they were still young, weren't they? They were poor and foreigners, but they were still young.

The party is held in the basement of a restaurant where there is a disco. As Agnes and Ruth make their entrance, the room turns to look, then returns to their conversations. The two girls stand at the entrance, as if suspended. Finally, well, this is BIZ-arre. Shall we? Agnes nods towards the bar. Ruth just keeps smoking her cigarette. Her face like smooth glass. She tries to affect Holly Golightly's stoicism when eating a croissant outside Tiffany's.

Near the bar Elspeth has cornered Olly. She is laughing at something he is saying and keeps on touching his arm, which holds a glass of beer, which Olly then lifts to his mouth, like a marionette. Agnes orders champagne and flirts with the bartender. Ruth lingers near her colleagues. Hi guys, she says. Elspeth smiles at Ruth. She was much friendlier now, ever since that day on the street. Hiya Ruth. Oh, hello, Ruth, says Olly, nicely. You look lovely. Ruth smiles, blushing. You look nice yourself. He is dressed in the same suit he wore at Horrids, but with a brightly colored necktie he had chosen for the occasion, a red that matches Agnes's hair.

Here you go. Agnes slides up behind them. Olly fixes his eyes on her red beam. She hands Ruth the other glass of champagne and Olly her hand, like she is in a movie about to be introduced to her leading man. My flatmate Agnes, Ruth, reluctantly. It's a pleasure, she purrs. Ruth actually feels sympathetic for Elspeth, who lingers at Olly's elbow, simmering. You're sitting with fragrance, aren't you? Elspeth pulling at his sleeve. Yes. Yes of course Olly smiles. He continues to stare mesmerized at Agnes. Would you ladies like to join us? He says to her. Elspeth smirks at Agnes. Oh, dear, there isn't room for *two* more. That's okay, Ruth says, apologetically. Olly finally excuses himself, following Elspeth's whip of black hair. Agnes grabs the crook of Ruth's arm, fingernails shoving in. Ouch Ruth winces. So that's Joan Crawford, hmmm? I guess Ruth says (thinking to herself, wouldn't Agnes be the femme fatale figure here?). If you're going to dye your hair black you at least have to wear lipstick, Agnes glares. So that's the infamous Olly. I guess, Ruth shrugs. Agnes has that look on her face, that look like she could eat glass. He would be so much fun to spoil, wouldn't he? She almost meows. Ruth doesn't know what to do but laugh. Why should Ruth be surprised? Or maybe the champagne tempered everything. If you want Olly, you're going to have to get through them, she nods her head at the table of girls, currently pawing at Olly like he is the homecoming king of Horrids. Those girls? They don't bother me, Agnes tosses her hair like an orange flame.

Dinner is an anonymous lump of meat smothered in brown gravy, vegetables tortured in a sauce of a similar shade. They are sitting alone. Agnes hadn't wanted to mingle. Ruth eats her champagne instead, watching the bubbles rise up, up, up, waving at a few of her colleagues, there's Ava Gardner, there's The Italian in men's fragrance who she has started taking smoke breaks with. Agnes eats her red lipstick, which she swirls and smacks with the ferocity of one going to battle. Like Mars, Ruth thinks.

People were starting to dance or pair off in the corners pressing up against each other. C'mon, Agnes pulls at her limp arm. Ruth teeters behind, splashing around her glass of sparkling blonde, a bemused look plastered on her face. Plastered. Agnes saunters up to Olly. The waves of girls separate. Dance with us she orders. Elspeth's white face looks pinched and pained. Olly stands up, yanked by the puppet strings attached around his penis.

Ruth stands on the edge of the dance floor, swaying, as Agnes circles around a hypnotized Olly, like predator around prey, grinding her hips. Agnes is such an imperialist, Ruth thinks fuzzily. The room dances around her. A man approaches her out of the corner of her eye. She vaguely recognizes him. Jimorsomething. From Cookery. He is saying something to her. So, what are your thoughts on the war?

Ruth regards him woozily. Is that, like, some sort of pick-up line?

He shrugs. She does not know if he is trying to flirt with her or be antagonistic. She sways back and forth slowly. She is annoyed. She doesn't answer him.

Now Jimorsomething from Cookery seems irritated. It is your president, you know. You voted for him.

Oh, okay. My green girl blinks. Blink, blink. Up, down the lashes.

She is frozen to the spot on the floor. She looks like one of those wax celebrities at Madame Tussauds. She eyes the bottom of her glass and ignores him, wishing him away. Someone has hit the mute button.

Hey, no worries. Cheers. And Jimorsomething from Cookery leaves her frame of vision.

She senses someone watching her from far away. The boy with the enflamed face. It embarrasses her, him seeing her drunk, but at least she won't remember tomorrow. For the rest of the evening the picture only worked in gasps and bursts. All faces blurred, racing. At some point a joint was offered. She accepted it, even though she was always a wreck when she drank and smoked at the same time. She accepted it all the same. Maybe she didn't know how to refuse. Or maybe it was that nihilist streak inside of herself that she could never understand, that impulse to ruin everything, to grind everything into its death. Or maybe it was Agnes? Maybe Agnes was the grand instigator of this entire collision? It was easier to blame Agnes. Yes, blame Agnes. Blame Agnes.

Such a gentleman to take us two unchaperoned ladies home. Agnes was doing all of the talking. Ruth was half-asleep, her head fallen into Agnes's scarlet lap. Agnes's cold pink fingers stroked her hair. The train's teeth grinded. Blame Agnes. Blame Agnes. This was a train crash waiting to happen. Above her she could make out slurping sounds. He doesn't know what he signed on for, Ruth thought. Do I? She drifted away into fuzziness.

And then she was on Agnes's bed, propped against the pillows. Her dress crumpled up on the floor. Her stockings had been ripped. She could just cry about those stockings. Agnes was kissing her, her tongue jetting in and out. Ruth kept gagging and pushing away. She couldn't breathe. The two girls were stripped down to their bra and panties. Ruth felt embarrassed by her cotton underwear against Agnes's red lace, also vaguely ashamed of the crotch-crust (what a dirty girl). Agnes was wearing Olly's red tie hooked loosely around her neck. Ruth craned her neck and saw Olly at the foot of the bed, dressed except with his penis in his hand. They were performing for him. He had said something about never having seen two girls together. Shooting two birds with one stone, something like that. It was all fun and games, all fun and games.

Agnes was struggling to remove Ruth's bra. No, no, please, Ruth whispered. Everything was spinning, spinning, spinning. She was on the ceiling, looking at the scene with a sort of horror, like slowing down mesmerized at the intimacy of a car crash, bodies torn, thrown against each other, their blood pooled together. Bodies and bodies.

They were all sprawled on the bed, the sheets twisted around their bodies. Allfunandgamesallfunandgames. Olly and Ruth were now kissing. Now Agnes was at the foot of her bed, on her knees, her lips gripped decidedly around Olly's penis, her face smeared with red like a rash.

And then Ruth was asleep on her mattress on the ground. She had begged off somehow. A brief flicker: Agnes and Olly still on the bed, above her, going at it, silently, as if not to wake the uninvited. Agnes is doubled over, as if praying, her hands grabbing the bedpost.

She wakes up with the entire world inside her mouth. She has the day off. That's the switch she'd like to push. Olly and Agnes are still asleep on Agnes's bed. The hurly-burly done. On tiptoes, Ruth quickly puts on yesterday's dress and, tying her coat around her waist, hurries downstairs, her chest about to explode, a nut of something in her throat choking her. She wore bare legs, perennially chafed and bruised. Her stockings were ripped. She could just cry about those stockings. As she opens the door she looks up to see a sleepy Agnes peering down from the banister. Her mascara splattered around her eyes, her hair knotted.

Where are you going? Agnes whispers hoarsely.

Out. Ruth whispers back. Fresh air.

Are you mad?

Pause. The nut loosens its hold in her throat. Why would I be mad?

Wait. Agnes tightens the sash of her satiny red robe and walks down the stairs so that she is inches away from Ruth. The bottoms of her feet black. What's wrong? she peers at her face closely.

Nothing. Ruth felt calm. She performs her magic trick of going dead inside.

Last night was pretty BIZ-arre. . . . Agnes surveys the ball of a sooty foot.

Yeah. They both half-smile. Ruth's face feels sore.

So, you and Olly. . . . Ruth breathes in. Is that what was bothering her?

Him? Her head snaps upstairs. She shrugs.

Oh. Well. I'm going to take off.

All right. Agnes yawns. Movie tonight?

Yeah. Maybe.

Agnes presses one finger to her lips, cracked with red, then touches Ruth's cheek.

Later, darling.

Ruth lifts her smirk weakly. Later.

— Listen…you know those days when you get the mean reds?
— The mean reds? You mean like the blues?
— No…the blues are because you're getting fat or because it's been raining too long. You're just sad, that's all. The mean reds are horrible. Suddenly you're afraid and you don't know what you're afraid of.

— Blake Edwards' *Breakfast at Tiffany's*

Everyone eventually disappoints me, thinks Ruth, escaping into the dirty streets. She doesn't feel equipped for outside, life streaming past in a palette of browns and grays, dotted with doomy rain, gloomy drain. The cold air baptizes her. Eyes squint against the sharp slap of wind, her face frozen with the harsh spit. She splashes through puddles, peering down alleys to make sure a moving vehicle does not rush out at her. The melancholy swoops down and lays on her flat. She feels exposed, like her skin has been torn off. No armor on today. Her legs are icicles. She feels furious at Agnes, furious at herself, that she allowed herself to be led a lamb to the slaughter. And also this sort of burning shame, of the horrors of last night, of how she behaved, of everything she let inside, of everything she had ever let inside.

She glares at single strollers who dare to look at her as they walk by. The world lay suspended in fog, along with the insides of her head. She journeys invisible through the fog. She puts on her sunglasses, masking melancholia. Crossing the road, a black cab looms out at her. She fixes her eyes on it. She intones out loud with the solemnity of a televangelist: Do Not Kill.

Will she cry in public? Is that a tear? We want to see her break down. We want to see her crack.

My icon of ruin. No hairline chips or cracks.

Is that a tear hurrying down her face? I taste it. I taste the salt of Ruth's tears. I confirm their veracity.

Heading into central London. Almost no passengers, a phantom train. A homeless man in a long filthy coat stands right in front of her, swaying on the silver pole. Ruth sits there with a ball of rage forming. I refuse to pay any attention to you. She fixes her gaze on the only other passengers, a couple in identical puffy white jackets folded into each other like hibernating bears. They are asleep, no witness to this attack on her privacy. The crazy man leans into her, muttering non-words. She knows what he is doing. She knows that everyone needs their own audience. But she refuses to play along, to act shocked or indignant or lash out at him. I refuse to look at you. She remains there frozen like a stone. I refuse to give you any attention, any crazy attention. Finally, he moves away, spluttering in frustration. She doesn't see him. He is not there. She keeps on playing back that scene from *The Big Sleep*. Did I hurt you much, sugar? The retort: You and every other man I've ever met. You and every other man I've ever met. Moans the train. You are every other man I've ever met.

A naked Olly looking through her at Agnes. Only at Agnes.

Roaming up and down the Tottenham Court beast, around and around, cheap Chinese and Indian buffets, banks, bus shelters advertising the latest Hollywood movie, the Scientology Center. Free Stress Tests reads the sign. Followers of L. Ron Hubbard stand outside, beckoning people in. They don't bother Ruth, which today mildly offends her. Maybe they don't think she is worthy of being saved. Maybe they see a girl who wants to fall.

Olly doubled over Agnes, silently, not wanting to wake the ghost asleep on the mattress. The ghost who was never there. Never really there.

I was never anything to you, was I? Nothing, nothing at all.

Veering around empty side streets. She smokes to avoid being alone. Gagging at cruel-sounding food posted on placards outside pubs sounds of body parts innards intestines photographs of pale plates of food Sausage Rolls BangersandMash SteakandKidneyPie BloodPudding ScotchEggs PickledEggs. Up back the belly of the beast. Charcoal of chestnuts, metal-boxed vendors. She walks into the Odeon to see what film was playing. She is greeted by a giantess with a prickly beard, who reminds Ruth of one of the monsters on *The Muppet Show*. A pang of guilt once the thought has settled somewhere. A Hollywood film began in thirty minutes, the bearded lady informs her. It is a romantic comedy with two comely attractive stars who fell in love with each other while filming and left their respective partners.

Do you talk of me to her? I beg you: not one word about us to those who come after me.

To fill time, she slips in and out of electronics shops on the street, walking by fast-moving images conjured up on large screens, not making eye contact with any of the salesmen whose eyes settle on her with desperation, canines dripping, a heart-thumping deer amidst a drought. She walks into grocery stores and flips through celebrity magazines and tabloids, IS SHE PREGGERS I LOST TEN STONE THE WEDDING PICTURES YOU HAVEN'T SEEN ignoring the watchful eye of the security guards.

Other names other faces. She'll put those on. She can take off her own and breathe.

Ruth wanders back into the theater, past the smell of burnt popcorn in the lobby. The bearded lady breaks her ticket in half. She sits in the center in the dark, staring at the wrinkled turquoise curtain. She touches her hand to her nose. It comes away dotted with a sticky red. Her nose is slightly bleeding. She wipes it with the back of her hand, a scarlet smear. There are two French children with their father in front of her, adult-sized popcorn bags the size of their insect-like torsos. They are a little young to be watching the movie. A little girl in knotty dishwater hair, a dirty white sweater with candy-colored hearts. Her brother starts sobbing. His father has refused him something. Ruth tries to drown out his childish gulps, fixating on the turquoise curtain. The adverts come on, the same for every movie she has seen in that theater. She laughs too hard at the automobile ads and mobile phone commercials, a tick of loneliness. She is advertising her own isolation.

Trudging home. Buskers at Tottenham Court Road. A man plays the theme song to *MASH* on his synthesizer. Near the stairs for the Central Line, a woman with long red hair and shearling boots pinches the harp to the clang of pence being occasionally dropped into her black case.

HE had always told her his dreams of taking off and playing music in the train stations of Europe. Rounding the corner or descending the steep elevator underground she always half-expected to see HIM picking away at a guitar with a furious expression on his face.

That empty feeling of listening to your own voice on an answering machine. That's what life is like for Ruth now. She pushes with the push of flesh climbing down the stairs to the platform, slowly moving, milling, careful not to trip.

I understand, all right. The hopeless dream of being—not seeming, but being. At every waking moment, alert. The gulf between what you are with others and what you are alone. The vertigo and the constant hunger to be exposed, to be seen through, perhaps even wiped out. Every inflection and every gesture a lie, every smile a grimace. Suicide? No, too vulgar. But you can refuse to move, refuse to talk, so that you don't have to lie. You can shut yourself in.

— Ingmar Bergman's *Persona*

The next morning she woke to a wet pillow, her eyes glaring like red light bulbs. Agnes had not come home the night before. Ruth calls in sick to work even though it was the week before the holidays. She knows that she could be sacked but she doesn't care.

She does not leave the house. She is in hiding. She hides because out there is too intense. The city a cruel hole with too many eyes. She sentences herself to a voluntary imprisonment. Lying on the mattress wanly watching the blur of Agnes's TV set, drooling catatonic onto her duvet, hand in her pajama bottoms. Making friends with the furballs under Agnes's bed.

Exclusive video: Ruth self-destructs.

Oh my Ruth how she suffers.

And yet, I am the one who is cruel. I experience joy at her suffering. I want to save her and then drown her like a surplus puppy.

She teeters between awake and asleep. When not sleeping she surrenders herself to a stream of images, festering and filling the room. She is incubating agitation. The weeping is back. The littlest things make her break down. She only gets up to make herself tea and shuffle back to her mattress. She aches terribly. The pain makes her unable to breathe. She cries out to herself in anguish:

I long for you. I can't stand it. I long for you. This thing inside, I can't get at it. I can't claw it away can't vomit it away can't drink it away. I want to destroy it. I want to destroy myself if that will destroy this thing inside. I imagine you everywhere. It hurts It hurts It hurts so fucking much this aching, this longing, this thing. And you feel nothing.

On days like this she cannot shower. She needs to collect, to accumulate. She needs to savor in her filmy layer. It is her protection against the world. To shower, a shock or a scream. Everything surrounding her she cannot wash away. To shower would be almost an admittance of a new day. To carry with her the same skin is to allow each day to blend into each other and be one day. The days will never end and neither will she. Days and days. No showering. She builds a protective armor. It's important, somehow, she knows. She cannot wash it away.

Collapsed on her mattress. She sleeps on magazines stuck to her thigh. She sleeps and sleeps and sinks and sleeps some more. Sedentary. Like grass, dirt, shoveling and shoveling and buried. She grows weak. She feels her muscles start to atrophy. She lies there with one hand down her front. What is she digging around there for. She takes it out occasionally and sniffs her warm sweaty palm, her animal scent.

She eats peanut butter sandwiches. Honey O's in cereal bowls gather at the foot of her mattress, the milk sour and congealed. Green and Black's chocolate bars, the chocolate smeared on her sheets.

Agnes returns. Ruth pretends not to notice. She tiptoes around Ruth, quiet so as not to disturb the disturbed, stepping over her, bangles jangling. Ruth prepares her defense in this trial inside of her mind.

I'm not crying over you. Do you think I'm crying over him? Don't be so arrogant. Do you think you're anything to me? You reminded me of someone else, that's all. You reminded me of someone else. I never chased after you, I never tried. I never wanted you. I merely wanted. That's the difference.

(Agnes and Ruth on stage, in between them a bemused Olly)
(Bleep) you (Bleep) you (Bleep) you.
Is that the best you got?
You took my man.
He wasn't your (bleep)ing man, he was nobody's (bleep)ing man, he wanted me more.
Maybe that's because you're such a (bleep)ing slut.
(Ruth throws a chair, Olly tries to hold off a furious Agnes. Bodyguards rush to the stage. The crowd goes wild. Pandemonium ensues.)

She wakes up to find a worried Agnes standing over her. Go away, she mumbles. This is how I choose to spend my holiday. Why couldn't anybody let her have a simple breakdown?

You need to get up.
I'm in a funk, Ruth explains. Ruth licks her lips. They were dry.
(*How is it that the clouds still hang on you*?)
Well, you need to snap yourself out of it.

Agnes still stands over her. Is this about the other night? Agnes refuses to budge. She feels guilty, Ruth realizes with surprise. It was not an emotion Ruth thought Agnes experienced. Ruth looks around Agnes, towards the flickering miniature people on the screen. Liz Taylor as Maggie-the-Cat begging Paul Newman to love her. I'm not living with you: We occupy the same cage, that's all. She imagines saying that to Agnes: We occupy the same cage, that's all.

Ruth sighs heavily. She feels deep inside that she hates Agnes. And that maybe Agnes harbors a greater hatred for her, a hate and a love both so intense it confuses her. It's just the holidays. I'll get over it.

The next time she looks up Agnes is gone.

I must get this crack mended.

— Catherine Deneuve in Roman Polanski's *Repulsion*

She knew what she had to do. Ruth stands in front of the mirror and studies herself.

She feels an immense violence stirring inside of her. She looks and looks in the mirror. She cannot find herself. She feels somewhere deep within a desire to cut through that glass, that image of herself. To explode outside of her small space. To destroy it somehow. To purge herself, cleanse herself, this creation, this product of others' eyes. To be wiped clean.

That itch, that desire to cut off one's hair, one's prize of ribbons, one's fire escape of femininity.

The green girl needs to externalize her own suffering. This is how she will wear her grief.

Or maybe she is just bored.

Or perhaps I am operating the strings. Perhaps I am directing this scene. Ruth is my silent film star, always silent on the outside even when she is screaming within. She is my Falconetti playing Joan of Arc.

I make my green girl kneel. I am the harsh director. She begs and pleads: Please don't make me do it but there is a clause in her contract. I am reminded of the Barbie dolls that I played with as a young girl. I would perform the cruelest acts on my lovelies. I would behead them. I would cut off their hair to make them look like Ken. I would sentence their bodies to various torture machines. Perhaps writing for me is an extension of playing with those dolls. Ruth is my doll. I crave to give birth to her and to commit unspeakable acts of violence against her. I feel twinges of joy at her suffering.

She looks at herself in the mirror. She looks at herself. She cannot break through. She stares at the haircutting shears resting at the sink, which Agnes uses to cut her fringe as well as her trim (brown as a mouse). She stares at the scissors and wills herself to pick them up.

Suddenly she picks up the scissors from the sink, grabbing a chunk of her hair. It does not cut as easily as she imagined.

She picks up the scissors and carves away at the girl with the blonde hair in the mirror.

She tears into her hair. She cuts and cuts and cuts. Clumps of blonde feathers come out in the sink. Her gorgeous virgin hair.

Is it masochistic? An act of self-flagellation. There is a finality to it. To cut off one's breasts in one mean gesture. To surrender oneself to vague and distant eyes. To say. This is the new me. I have been born clean. See my face. I wipe the paint from the mouth of the pretty girl. Wipe the paint from your mouth. This is me. I have no shield of feathers to hide behind. I am ugly and true. I have cut off my lovely, my darling. Cut it off. Cut, cut, it off. I stand a monument to pain. I stand naked to this world.

When Mia Farrow cut her hair off, Salvador Dali called it "mythical suicide." What happens to a woman when the eyes are no longer on her? Is that in a way a tiny death? Or a sort of freedom? The locks shorn off. Is one unlocked? The rape of her locks.

Now, a close-up on her face. Her face haunting, haunted. The tears begin to tumble out a torrential rain.

Although she is sobbing still she attacks her hair. More. More. After a few minutes of frenzied ecstatic cutting she examines herself. Hanging on to the porcelain sink stained like dried blood with Agnes's hair dye, which tilts as she leans.

First the dread sets in. She begins to grieve her hair with genuine sorrow.

She lays herself down on her sea of clothes, her own chalk outline. She spreads her arms wide, a banal crucifixion. Oh, she is ugly. She is ugly, ugly, ugly.

O the horror the horror. And nothing to be done.

Then she curiously feels calm. And numb. And her head proud and cold, like a Greek statue. Like she is wiped clean.

Finally Ruth manages to rouse herself. She showers and dresses in an armory of black wilted fabric. She cleans and powders her face and surveys the damage. She combs what was left of her hair carefully. She painstakingly applies her makeup, taking no pleasure, no love, in painting her face. It is her mask to shield her from the day, the world. Two dots of pink blush on each cheek, a stroke of black mascara, a protective coat of pink lip gloss.

She meditates in the mirror. She gets lost trying to pluck her single blond hair on her neck. It comforts her, feeling it, tickling it, trying to catch it. The tweezer leaves a map of red prick marks on the side of her pale neck.

Finally she picks up her phone. Almost coolly, calmly. The mask back on. She schedules an appointment with a salon down the road.

She stumbles out a fetus into the cold air, her beret covering her science experiment. The salon is off a side street on Brick Lane. She opens the glass door. Bored swiveled eyes, returning disappointed.

Hi, I'm Ruth. I've a 2 p.m.

A gangly boy stands up from his previous place lying down on the sofa covered with customers' coats. He wears black sweatbands on each wrist. She follows him downstairs to a room of lonely disembodied sinks. She lays her head back onto the hard curve, her legs sticking out. The hose rushing out too hot, too cold, just right. The water swishes in her ear. When he touches her hair, tears come to Ruth's eyes. It feels like so long since she had last been touched with purpose.

Big plans for tonight?

No, no. Just staying in. Soft, breathy. She couldn't remember how to talk, how to socialize outside of her head.

Cool, cool. She struggles up. He dabs at her with a cheap white towel, which he arranges around her neck. Like a boxer between rounds. She follows him, fragile and exposed, up the winding stairs, nervously nodding to Michael Jackson's "Thriller."

She follows the boy to a chair. There is no mirror. He fits her around the neck with the uniform black shroud. He nods at the stylist, a bored-looking Scottish woman, and returns to his post, body down on the sofa.

Tried to cut your own hair, hmmm? She lights a cigarette, running her hands through the damage, lifting up a black cowboy boot to pump her up higher in the air.

Yes. She has turned to stone. She doesn't want to talk about it.

It looks terrible, doesn't it? Ruth then gulps. She can't see herself. How does she know that she exists if she can't see herself?

The woman shrugs. What were you trying to do? She is wearing tight black jeans, from which a pouch of white flesh spills out.

Have you seen *Breathless*?

Nope.

Jean Seberg?

Suck, exhale, blank expression. She places her cigarette in the filled ashtray. It simmers along with others extinguished and estranged.

I thought it would be freeing. (I wanted to be clean. Wiped clean.)

Eyebrow cocked. More flipping through hair, looking to see how it falls. She was a woman of few words.

Just don't make me completely bald.

The woman snorts. You did a pretty good job of that yourself. She lights another cigarette.

You want me to take it all off? Like short short?

Yes. Yes. Take it off. Take it all off.

She shrugs again.

Ruth busies herself with a magazine on her lap. Flip flip flip. Beautifulwomenbeautifulclothes. Everyone in the magazine has long hair. Long, long, lovely hair. She feels fragmented. She forgets who she is. She forgets who she was. Filled again with that destructive sense of want. Of want and can't have. A damp blonde rain falls onto flaxen-haired maidens in party dresses. They are all lying in a bed of hay, as if they had accidentally fallen there. Ticklish, Ruth's hair sticks, to her face, her lips, her lap, the girls' pouty faces.

The whiz of a razor being applied to Ruth's neck, to the sides of her head. She looked at the woman next to her. An older woman with silver foil in dark wettened hair. She overhears her talking to her stylist, a boy with a rat's tail down his neck and tight jeans. Ruth can make out snippets. I suspect. I suppose. Oh dear.

The whir of hairdryers.

Ruth relaxes into blankness. She turns into a stone statue.

Whaddya think? Hand mirror handed over.

A more glamorous alien blinked back at her. Her eyes were planets. Big beautiful glassy eyes offset by a startle of lashes.

Oh. She gasps.

What's the matter.

I don't recognize myself.

I think it looks brilliant. The woman lights another cigarette, the former abandoned to the heap of half-formed bodies. It really brings out your bone structure.

Everyone in the shop turns towards her. Who is that girl? You've got a wonderful head, the boy from the couch says. Thank you, she murmurs. She can feel others looking.

Walking home, she catches flashes of the unfamiliar girl in shop windows. She is unable to tear her eyes away. She poses for invisible cameras. She knows her angles. Her best sides. She keeps on patting her head, rubbing her hand back and forth. She likes the feel of it. Soft and fuzzy like a baby chick.

Agnes is smoking and watching TV when Ruth makes her entrance. Ruth hasn't seen her in what seems like forever. She stands there waiting for her to notice that she is there.

Agnes finally looks up.

I got my hair cut.

I see. Agnes at a rare loss for words. Finally she springs up from the bed to touch Ruth's blonde globe. She runs her fingers through it critically.

Mia Farrow, *Rosemary's Baby*. Ruth Gordon feeding you tanas root.

I was going for Jean Seberg.

New York Herald Tribune!

Something like that.

Wow. Agnes marvels. Now you're interesting. You were a bit dull before.

Thanks. I think.

No, really, you've just changed everything.

Agnes steps back, as if to appraise her from afar. You look like a charming little boy.

Thanks a lot, Agnes.

Gawd. That's a compliment. Androgyny is very in fashion, you know.

Ruth locks herself in the bathroom. She wants to be alone with her new self. Entranced by this strange girl in the mirror. With her radical crop she has made a radical alteration. She has cut away her old self.

Everyone in her department has to do a double-take upon her return. Oh, you cut your hair! You cut your hair! You look like a little French gamine says The Italian.

What would HE say. The shock of the new.
You cut your hair.
I know.

Whenever she saw Olly's approach she would stare him down with emboldened eyes, her Medusa mask, daring him to say anything, anything to her or anybody else for that matter on any subject concerning her. He would inevitably scurry away, scared off by her calm eyes, her unblinking fury.

At the café. A man stops in front of her table. He looks at her as if trying to decipher something. Finally he snaps his fingers and points at her:

Bonjour Tristesse! he says.

Yes she says. Modestly, eyes lowered, surrendering herself to his insatiable gaze.

Through the sad heart of Ruth, when, sick for home, she
stood in tears amidst the alien corn.

— John Keats, "Ode to a Nightingale"

Ruth, Ruth, I need you. All of a sudden Noncy is in front of her and clasping Ruth's wrist with her fingers. She had long cold fingers like Ruth imagined a Victorian heiress would have. Fragile and frazzled, like Vivien Leigh playing Blanche DuBois in *A Streetcar Named Desire.*

Desire, would you care to try? Desire? Desire?

You need to work the till today. Right now? Noncy sighs loudly. There's a queue forming and I need you to ring up customers with Elspeth. Ruth, are you listening?

Oh. Okay. She smiles.

Noncy sighs, then attempts a smile back, although it looks more like a grimace. Ta.

Ta! Ta! Ta! This was a word Ruth heard everywhere at Horrids. She assumed at first it was the English clearing their throat at the end of a sentence. But Agnes had informed her that it was actually shorthand for thanks. But, like cheers, it was an English mannerism Ruth could not bring herself to affect, knowing that it would cement her position as a foreigner even further.

Ta, Elspeth smiles weakly, as Ruth hurries over to help her, wrapping up boxes of perfume in paper, placing them in the shiny Horrids bag.

It's all right she says although it is impossible to hear her over the din. itsallright.

She began to take smoke breaks with The Italian. The Italian, blowing out reams of grayish agitation. He was a dramatic smoker, could communicate emotions with that interplay of cigarette and smoke and mouth and flame that his sticky English could not, like Ava Gardner with her dark expressive eyes. It's cold cold, she brr brred. The weather in London was The Italian's favorite topic, she knew. Oh, his face snarled up. Tap tap went the cigarette furiously accompanying his frantic foot well embraced in designer leather. He waved his cigarette-holding hand as he talked, pausing at times to inhale with delight, pausing for the smoke to circulate around his Flungs, and then breathing out again for emphasis. He was a famous tenor mourning over his fallen soprano. He was Othello mourning his Desdemona. He was Desdemona. He was *Swan Lake.* She watched enraptured at his performance.

I am miserable, Ruth. This weather—so bad. I hate it so much. Quick gulp of smoke and blow out of air. It's so fucking dark and cold. This shit cold is killing me. I miss the beach I miss the sun I miss light and life, you know?

It hasn't even snowed, Ruth sighs the chorus. She licks her upper lip, tastes the tang, wonders whether it's stained yellow.

Snow? No, that would be beautiful. That would be white and it would settle somewhere and would be beautiful. No, this is just gray. His face twists elegantly digesting the smoke. This is death. I am going to die here, Ruth. A twist more of pathos. Ruth laughs. You are so melodramatic, she tells him.

He flutters his hand against his forehead. I miss Italy so much. Like a lover.

Do you miss the States? The Italian asks her.

What a question. No. Too quick an answer. Then she thinks about it, licking the tip of her browning filter. Not really. Not the country. Maybe some people inside the country. But the mass of land, no, I do not miss.

But your president you miss? He could just never forgive her for being an American. She would always be to him his American friend. Like an exotic pet.

Oh yes, desperately. She shoots him daggers. He laughs. He continues to goad her. This was his favorite routine.

But you voted for him, no?

No, I told you, I didn't vote. They had had this same conversation many times.

But that is unforgivable, no? That is the same as inviting him into your bed.

I've invited worse. She is playing tough-talker. A modern-day Veronica Lake.

Ugghh. That's disgusting. I would not fuck your monkey of a president for one million pounds. Such a macho cowboy murderer. The Italian got as heated talking about politics as talking about the weather. Now your Bill Clinton, that's another story.

How about Blair? The Italian thinks about it, shrugging, a reluctant, teasing smile. Maybe. For one million.

Ewww. Those ears. Ruth erupts into giggles.

The horrible head pops his head out, a tanned mask of disgust. He hated the smokers. Thought their need for breaks a weakness not fitting of the Horrids employ. As he turned his head around The Italian flicks his dead cigarette in his direction, an impotent gesture of revolt.

How about him? She nods at the back of the horrible head, while hurriedly finishing her cigarette, twisting her foot on its broken back.

The Italian groans. Not for all the money in the world. You?

Ruth mock-considers this. I don't know. There's something about a powerful man that's very sexy.

You find him sexy? The Italian, incredulous.

I didn't say that. But people are quite different when they've taken off their business suit.

You would have to be on top. The Italian mimes a large stomach.

Are you kidding? I would insist on it.

Strutting in like they own the place, still in hysterics, much to the puzzlement of the English everyone else around them.

She began to work the till more. She enjoyed working the till, although that meant she had to interact with people more often. It was easier if she played a part.

Next please. Next please.

She liked handling the bank notes, almost like playing with pastel paper money. At the cling of the cash drawer the Queens staring haughtily in succession. Blue-green queen, orange, pink-purple. Ringlets, tiara and stern expression. Once in a while Ruth would turn one over as if to disobey.

She enjoyed watching customers sign their names on their credit card slips. Those carefully rehearsed scrawls of identity. Some pens swoop in from the left, thick fingers clutching on. Some signatures look as mysterious as writing in the air before the smoke clears and the outline can be deciphered. Others reveal the subconscious cement of elementary school, the careful curlicue unable to be freed, even if the writer of the childish signature has taken drugs, gone to bed with numerous people, entertained generally illicit and immoral thoughts, all to rid themselves of the spectre of good penmanship.

She admired the women's handsome leather wallets, metal clasps sprung open to reveal credit cards and coins of gold. Their glossy nails made her embarrassed of her rough palms, her ragged edges.

After an eternal shift Ruth walks home in gloom. The nag of another headache. Maybe she forgot to eat. The busker with the kung-fu mustache played an off-key "Auld Lang Syne." May all acquaintance be forgot, and never come to mind.

She thinks about HIM, HE who always occupies her thoughts in the complex of her mind, HE who has ruined her for all men who might come after, HE whom she obsesses over.

I need to forget you. I need you to release me. We'll be shadows to each other from now on, shadows of a former life. A shadow bears no scars.

The way home, the night is so clear, Ruth can see the tops of buildings she didn't know existed. So clear she can almost make out the smooth ornament of the Gherkin off in the distance when exiting the station, a glistening window-paned egg. 40p man still nowhere to be seen. Turning towards the market, snow began to fall, thin belts of fluff. It's snowing! A girl yells into her mobile. Spitalfields Church glowed like a phantom dog on its haunches.

Agnes is not home again. Ruth lies on her mattress. She plays dead and tries to ignore the sounds outside, the terribleness and teem of holiday-makers pouring down the street, loose with drink and an arrogant conviction that there is nothing else going on in that corner of the world besides their celebrations, no one trying to sleep, no dark nights of the soul.

Will you please just give me 40 bloody p? 40p man was back like a vengeful ghost. Lately he had become irate, a wildly circulating storm. Ruth didn't know what propelled this suddenly violent need (or maybe she did) but she began walking down other side streets when she glimpsed his shadow.

I'm talking to you.
Don't you dare ignore me.
Don't you dare ignore me.

We'd often go to the movies. We'd shiver as the screen lit up. But more often, Madeleine and I would be disappointed. More often we'd be disappointed. The images flickered. Marilyn Monroe looked terribly old. It saddened us. It wasn't the film we had dreamed, the film we all carried in our hearts, the film we wanted to make...and secretly wanted to live.

— Jean-Luc Godard's *Masculin féminin*

A celebrity was coming to preside over the Horrids after-holiday sale. It had been announced in all of the papers. SHE is an American television actress. The show SHE is on is popular over here too.

Ruth had often seen HER face peering at her from newsagents, along with the rest of HER body, clothed only in lingerie and arranged in a seductive manner on the covers of lads' magazines. With a look that reads *I want you but you can't afford me.*

Of course one cannot touch HER because she is a celebrity, a distant deity, a star. Stars are meant to show us how dull and dirty our lives are by comparison. And yet we want to be near THEM, be near their glowing light, their solar power. We are invisible yet THEY are highly visible. THEY are a known known, and we are an unknown unknown, sometimes even to ourselves.

All are waiting breathless with anticipation for HER arrival. It will be fan-demonium. It is like royalty is coming. Royalty IS coming—for SHE is a star, and SHE was gracing them with her presence.

It was all anyone could talk about for the preceding days. Oh, I just love HER says The Italian. They gossip about HER personal life, which they know intimately, after reading HER life story spelled out in all of the tabloids, who SHE dated, who SHE bedded, what kind of lipstick SHE uses.

They cleaned and cleaned for HER arrival. They made everything sparkly and shiny and bright.

They lay in wait. There are cameras and press salivating to document HER every rehearsed move. It is a feeding frenzy. They feed on celebrity. Everyone is beside themselves. Celebrity is a drug we take, only afterwards we realize we are ugly and no one loves us. We are deadened by these images, flattened into insignificance. Yet we will get down on our knees and worship HER, for SHE is beautiful and famous and hence very special in the universe.

There is a different feeling to the room. SHE is about to arrive. SHE has arrived. SHE does not disappoint, unlike ourselves and other people in our lives, who disappoint us all the time. SHE arrives in a horse and carriage. All the accompanying livery. SHE is wearing an all-white pantsuit, a very expensive designer no doubt. SHE is tinier than she appears on TV yet has a large head, which is the key to telegenic success. SHE is a vision, a vision of perfection, HER hair out of a shampoo commercial, HER face out of a cosmetics ad. We see HER face when SHE takes off HER designer Dior sunglasses. Which are very different from Ruth's sunglasses, which look like movie star sunglasses but are cheap and plastic and from Topshop. It is hot in the sun of celebrity, what with all of the adoring eyes and the camera flashes. That is why so many Hollywood celebrities are tan.

SHE enters with HER arm tucked into the arm of the horrible head. Everyone parts for HER, for the white orb of light. SHE waves, SHE giggles something indistinct into the horrible head's ear, he pats HER hand reassuringly. SHE poses for a few pictures. SHE leaves. That is all. And when SHE leaves everyone sighs and goes back to their ordinary lives and feels somewhat emptier, slinking past their mirror images, unsure of how to put together the puzzle pieces to make themselves feel whole.

When Ruth witnesses the grand entrance of the television actress, for just a brief flicker she imagines herself amidst the spectacle. It is RUTH who is on the arm of the horrible head. RUTH graciously signing her name to a row of grasping hands, nameless faces. It is RUTH who is wanted. RUTH who is adored. It is the curve of RUTH's face that is memorized, that is known.

The world diagnoses her as being young and lovely and a tad mysterious. She is elusive, playful, a cipher. She knows how to be stared at. She sits in cafes, in trains, and lets the gaze of the world bathe her. She turns her neck from side to side for a different view.

Ruth. Ruth the golden girl the cover girl the girl next door the girl on the moon. Time has been good to Ruth life goes where she does. She has been profiled, covered, revealed, reported on, what she eats, and what she wears, who she knows and where she was and when and where she's going.

Ruth. You know all about Ruth.

Exclusive video: RUTH. RUTH steps out of a cab. Legs first, then the rest of her. Flashes! Pop! Pop! The sunglasses shield her from the paparazzi. The camera bulbs are hot.

The sunglasses come off. There's a camera. She smiles. She waves.

RUTH! RUTH! Over here! Over here!

The sale people come out for the sale. Sale people are the worst kind of people. They maul through the carefully set up boxes of discount merchandise. They are gross specimens. They are not beautiful people. Some of them are fat. American fat. Talk-show fat. They mill about greedy monsters, hopeful monsters, lusty for that elusive find.

The ride home, the train stops suddenly in a dark tunnel. Ruth examines her fellow passengers in the empty car, measuring them up. A large woman in a cornflower blue housedress stares suspiciously at Ruth. Her shopping bags lean into her pantyhose-wrinkled ankles like expressionless pets.

A curly-haired man looks directly at her. He has been ambling around the platform before the train came, muttering to himself, spitting into the dark void of the tracks. Ruth had avoided him for fear that he might push her in front of the train tracks. Nutters here, or mental. Now she kept her face frozen, immobile.

These, the last human beings she will ever see.

The car remains stopped in silence.

The train begins to move, as if it was just clearing its throat, as if it had never halted in its journey.

Someone probably killed themselves on the tracks, Agnes declared, all nonchalance, after Ruth complained of the stalled train. People do that? Ruth wondered. A shiver went through her.

The next morning she aligned her toes against the painted yellow line. She stared into the guts of the tracks, as if mesmerized. She saw her reflection passing, passing her by in the glass of the incoming train.

Doors opening.

Mind the gap.

First of all, I must make it clear that this girl does not know herself apart from the fact that she goes on living aimlessly. Were she foolish enough to ask herself "Who am I?" she would fall flat on her face. For the question "Who am I?" creates a need. And how does one satisfy that need? To probe oneself is to recognize that one is incomplete.

— Clarice Lispector, *The Hour of the Star*

Why did you cut your hair? She is taking her break with Rhys, the boy with the enflamed face.

All about the massive food hall, this chaotic Emerald City, shoppers are milling about greedily. Shouting orders to the gourmet cheese counter, the gourmet tropical fruit counter. It was the Epcot Center of food—let's visit France, Italy, then Asia. Hungry bodies thronged all about them, standing in the queue at the bakery for bread, lumpy asses pressed against each other at the sushi bar, cramming monster sandwiches made of piles of red-tinged meat down their throats at the gourmet deli, children with bodies like insects begging for gummies arranged in every color, for bars of chocolate bigger than their heads, children threatening to burst with the full force of their tantrums if they are denied. Mummy! Mommy! Please! Please! A little girl of unknown nationality is on her knees, screaming bloody murder as her mother tries to pull her little arm away from the old-fashioned soda fountain where happier, more or less well-behaved children are receiving melting balls of ice cream piled on top of each other in a melting orgy. She screams and screams. Her face turns every color of the rainbow just like the ice cream denied to her. Her mother folds her arms and watches. This is a parenting technique.

But in the still center sit Ruth and Rhys with coffees in front of them. He seems so nice, so sensitive, such a nice boy.

All that exists is the two of them, in that moment. Something very important is happening. They are hungry for something else, something deeper. Ruth knows that this is an important interview. She gazes at his hopeful face. She sees him looking at her with an intensity that frightens and flatters her. She likes what he sees when he looks at her.

Why did I cut my hair? She pats her head nervously, as if startled to find it had disappeared in the middle of the night. You don't like it?

He regards her seriously. He is always serious. Their interaction was always serious, from the beginning.

You look like Joan of Arc.

Thanks, she says. She smiles dutifully at the compliment.

I see a deep pain inside of you the boy with the enflamed face is now saying.

You do? Ruth does not know anymore whether his face is hers or her face is his. His eyes were her eyes. She is intoxicated by his worshipful gaze. She sits greedy for attention, gobbling it up.

He nods. He takes her seriously. He listens to her. He understands.

She sees that he sees her, sees something pure and good in her. She wants to be that, wants to be pure and good again for him. She senses that he wants to save her somehow, save her from herself. Save her from the noise, the commotion, the chaos. (A green girl necessarily needs a Savior.)

I guess, everything felt so out of control and this made me feel less chaotic. Does that make sense? He nods again. His gentle, pained face understands. There is something almost too good about him, that repels Ruth. With her simultaneous desire to be good for him is another desire to ruin him along with herself. But she does not understand this. She just acts. She just reacts.

You know Catherine of Siena cut her hair to be closer to God.

I don't think that's why I did it, Ruth giggles. She tries to act serious again when she sees Rhys doesn't find this funny.

He begins telling her that Catherine of Siena's family had problems with her ascetism, her refusal to consider a proper marriage. She would fast from a young age, she would deprive herself of sleep. As he lectures her Ruth suddenly notices how skinny Rhys is, his slender arms, his long bony hands like an Egon Schiele figure. His eyes were red-rimmed, exhausted. She had a sudden desire to hold him in her arms, to nurse him back to health, to mother him.

I think I remembered that from Catholic school. When I was little I loved learning about the saints. My favorite was St. Lucy.

Why? His eyes regard her. His eyes were the clearest, unmilkiest blue. A blue like a newborn's. A blue that shot right through her. The lovely Lucy with the lovely golden hair, who took out her eyeballs for a suitor, who said here, you can have them if you think they are so lovely.

Oh, I don't know. She was so young and beautiful. And she was a martyr, right? Her habit of asking permission with every comment.

And she was stoned to death, right?

Rhys nods.

I wanted to marry God when I got my First Communion.

She has again amused him. You did?

Oh, yeah. I just was filled with such love for God, and I wanted to marry him and be a nun and just worship him. I remember kneeling on those hard wooden pews and the red impressions they would leave on my knees and thinking how much I wanted to be his bride. I was like nine or something.

What happened?

I don't know. I discovered boys, I guess.

Rhys continues his lecture. He tells her that Catherine of Siena had a mystical marriage with God. She received an invisible wedding ring from the Infant Jesus. She described her unions with him, her raptures, in extremely erotic language.

That's interesting. Says Ruth. This is what she says when she's not terribly interested. It is also what she says when she is interested, but has nothing to add.

Many medieval mystics received visions. They described these states of utter abandon, and then the Lord would enter them and they were filled with the spirit and it would produce a joy so sublime that it was impossible to describe.

You're really interested in this. Ruth's coffee was cold. She drank it anyway. But only a bit at a time, little sips, because her eyes were still locked in with Rhys's.

I went to divinity school for a while.

Oh. Ruth doesn't know what to say.

Rhys and she both stare at their coffee.

I took some time off, he finally says. I'm living with my parents.

Oh. This surprises Ruth but she does not say anything else.

After another awkward pause Rhys continues. Ruth lets him. Catherine of Siena found joy in torturing her body. His eyes light up. She thought her suffering was a service to God. She would bathe lepers' feet and then drink the water. She would drink pus. She scalded herself. Or St. Veronica would eat cobwebs. Catherine of Genoa would bite or burn herself in trances. She would eat scabs and lice.

Gross. Ruth looks at the heaving mass of a man next to them shoving an egg roll down his throat, licking brown sauce off his fingers. Were they crazy? Why would they do that?

Rhys sighs, as if he's disappointed with her. Ruth watches his long bony fingers temple his cup. But he still looks like he has already forgiven her. He starts talking again. Ruth tries to pay attention. She wants to be a good student. Rhys grows increasingly excited. They wanted to experience Christ's suffering. They wanted to repeat his torture. They abandoned themselves to God through this mortification of their flesh. It's how they annihilated themselves. Angela of Foligno told her confessor—I could not imagine a death vile enough to match my desire. They wanted to find transcendence. They wanted to escape the cages of their bodies and be at one with God.

Oh. Ruth is made uncomfortable by the direct beam of his gaze. There was something almost fanatical about Rhys.

So, are you really religious? she finally asks.

His long fingers continue to choke his coffee cup. These women just really fascinate me. Their fervor. After these visions they would experience such excruciating pain and longing at God's departure. What would it be like—to feel something that intensely?

Yeah. Ruth actually does understand but doesn't know how to say this. She feels she knows what he means. That's really interesting she says. She doesn't know why she keeps on saying that. She hates how inarticulate she's being.

Well. Rhys checks his watch fastened to his bony wrist. I've got to get back on the floor. He fixes her again with that gaze as he takes her coffee cup to throw away along with his. Can I see you again?

Yes. Ruth says. Yes. Yes. There was so much more to say. She hadn't talked nearly enough about herself.

I must confess that, in allowing this man to return tomorrow, I was giving way to my desire to keep, not an admirer, not a friend, but an eager spectator of my life and person.

— Colette, *The Vagabonde*

Perhaps, ever since Ruth had arrived in London, she was looking for a vessel in which to pour out her confessions. Maybe this was what she was searching for, if she was searching for anything at all, an ear in which to whisper: I have experienced loss, just an ear, not even a person attached. I have experienced loss. She had not found the right person to possess such information. Not even Agnes knew Ruth's mother was dead, because Agnes never asked, and Ruth never told her.

From the moment they first met she sensed Rhys would listen to her.

My mother is dead. She now tells him. They are at the French café. This is the second round of interviews. The waiter is making fluttering eyes at him.

When she says these words out loud a relief comes, a relief in the form of tears, which she wipes away hurriedly with her napkin. She stares at her lap for a moment.

To say it makes it real.

Rhys nods. He understands. His gentle, pained face understands.

He doesn't say anything. He waits for her to speak.

I have experienced loss, she now says. But she is now thinking of HIM, not her mother. HE who haunts her thoughts.

I long for you. I can't stand it. I long for you.

Rhys moves his chair over closer to her. He dries her tears now with his napkin, now splattered with dark mascara. He cleans her face. He looks into her eyes. His face is love.

You loved your mother. That is a beautiful thing.

Yes. I loved my mother. Oh how I loved her. I didn't think I possessed such reservoirs of love.

They began to meet up everywhere. They ate lunch together. He walked her home from work. They held hands and kissed but never touched beyond that. She was exhausted after their sessions. Time would pass in this intense state and she would look up and it would be night out. They held hands through dark and scary streets. He protected her from the eyes of others. When she was with him she felt less afraid. When she was with him she was as innocent as he was.

There was a tenderness to the way her Prince Myshkin treated her, a carefulness verging on devoutness.

She found herself confessing everything to him, telling him her life story, which, besides the death of her mother, was the usual list of traumas self-inflicted. She slices her wrists and pours out pieces of herself all over the table. She shows him her scars. She tells him of HIM. Of all the HIMs before. Of everything foul and evil she had ever let inside of her. She is Mary Magdalene pressing her perfumed hair onto his feet. He wants to save this fallen angel.

She had so many questions so many questions.

They are walking amidst crowds in central London. Her arm is grasped around his slender waist as if she is holding on for support.

Past the crush on Carnaby, a maze of umbrellas and shopping bags.

Will I know her afterwards? They have had this debate several times before. She is always dissatisfied with his answer.

Rhys is patient, gentle. I just don't think it works like that, Ruth.

Why not? She presses.

I just don't think it does.

Why? She is a child, she asks this over and over again. Why? Why?

He sighs. It is beginning to rain, an annoying tinkle, like insects against their faces. It's a bit closed-minded to think that…

What?

That you live this embodied existence afterwards…

Ruth persists. But do you believe in an afterlife?

I'm not sure.

Down Oxford Street, they stop to watch the Hare Krishnas parading slowly up the other end of the street. Ruth stops and claps gleefully. Rhys is amused.

There has to be, doesn't there? Ruth continues. There has to be? What's the use of it all then if nothing happens?

I don't know, says Rhys.

I want to talk in the afterlife, Ruth says.

I don't think souls talk. Things are more transcendent.

They pass a hen party waiting to cross Oxford Street, women wearing veils decorated with toy penises.

Transcendent sounds boring, Ruth pouts.

The crush of bodies on Charing Cross Road. Tickets for Electric Six! a man with a Cockney accent, hands in pocket, strolls by. Past a field of Mohawks like roosters.

Simone Weil says we need to let go of our ego. You must forget I. Says Rhys.

They shake their heads no to the smocked girl standing outside an overpriced pizza place, holding a metal pizza tray on which remnants of a cheesy carcass rested. They pass alleys with their human stink.

They shake their heads, sorry, no, to the skinny homeless girl who sits on a blanket outside Sainsbury's, clothed in flannel surrounded by a cloud of smoke. With a mournful expression on her sooty face she holds up a sign. Help me. To complete the picture is her three-legged golden retriever, fur spiky from lack of wash, limping near an overflowing trash bin, his bandaged half-limb now blackened.

They are at home, sitting on Ruth's mattress, facing each other. I need I says Ruth. I am all I have.

But sometimes I am so crazed with love
I do not know what I am saying.

— St. Teresa of Avila

He began to stay the night when Agnes wasn't home, which was often. He would hold her while she wept.

I'm scared of dying.
Sh, sh, it's okay.

He cradles her, his body long and tender, as they listen to a man being beaten up on the street.

Oh, Ruth. He murmurs into her hair. How you've suffered.

That night is the first night Ruth tries to defile Rhys. She pins his pale arms down. She sees herself in his eyes, liquid shadows of self, twisting and turning. There was something so virginal and pure about him that she wanted to soil.

Ruth I love you but no he says.

Sometimes, as a cruel consolation prize, he lets her put makeup on him, blue eyeshadow grotesquely highlighting those blue eyes, a bit of red lipstick, and she would laugh and laugh at how pretty he was, her solemn philosopher.

On a rare night when she is not attached to Rhys's side and Agnes was home, the two girls lie around together and participate in their favorite mutual activity—the grooming of themselves. Things are still strange between them, Ruth can tell, they are not really talking, but they don't talk about this either. Agnes is in her red robe, sitting on their dusty floor at the top of the stairs, squinting in concentration, cigarette in her mouth, attempting to paint her toenails black. Her red robe billowed open so that her large breasts occasionally pop out, revealing her large red nipples that always look somehow surprised, more vulnerable than Agnes herself allowed (in contrast, Ruth's slightly lopsided small breasts with their hard brown nips always look annoyed at something). Agnes is doing a sloppy job painting her toenails, because she isn't paying enough attention and keeps on dripping the nail polish on the floor, attempting to slide away the errant glop on her toes with her blackened fingernail moon.

Ruth is sitting on the mattress and gripping her left big toe close to her face, attempting to cut out her ingrown toenail with a slightly rusty clipper. She can do this for hours. Just tunnel in, cut and cut extra skin, until at the end her toe is a bloody mess. It is deeply soothing.

Ruth takes a break and opens up the book of Teresa of Avila's confessions that Rhys has given her. (He is always giving her books to read.) She had already gotten various stains on the Penguin paperback bearing Bernini's statue on the cover (chocolate, now blood, god, she is so gross). Listen to this, she says to Agnes, who is now attempting to remove some of the goopy black with a cotton pad, which becomes embedded in dry puffs in the polish, syncopating this stage with the occasional expletive and hoarse cough. (Agnes is coming down with a cold, that evening she had already showed Ruth the puss pockets at the back of her throat, which grosses Ruth out, which Agnes delights in.)

I am certain that the pain penetrated my deepest entrails and it seemed if they were torn when my spiritual spouse withdrew the arrow with which he had penetrated them.

That's fucked up. Agnes coughs. She then spits out yellow phlegm into one of the cotton pads, looks at it and wrinkles her nose (gross) before folding up the pad and throwing it along with the blackened others. What is that?

It's Teresa of Avila.

What a whore.

Ruth smirks.

Agnes stretches out her legs, bobbing them up and down slightly, frowning at her shitty paint job. He gave that to you? Sometimes they were over, watching a movie, while Agnes was getting ready to leave for the night. Ruth could tell Agnes didn't like Rhys (she never called him by name, for one, but then she never called any boys by name) although she also felt that Agnes wouldn't like anyone Ruth was with, she didn't really know why, or maybe she did. Something to do with jealousy. Also, Agnes was a bitch.

Are you two finally . . . fucking? Ruth watches Agnes light a cigarette.

Ruth sighs, picks up her toe again, contorts herself. Noooo . . . she says. He respects me too much.

Is he not attracted to girls? Or to you? Agnes ashes accidentally onto her robe, which she wipes away, leaving a gray smear.

I don't know. I . . . think he is. Ruth looks down at her mangled toe again, fingering it. She wonders if Agnes is purposefully trying to make her feel bad.

Agnes snorts. Then coughs again, chestily. BIZ-arre. Maybe you should read him some of that stuff first.

Ruth giggles. She can't help but find Agnes amusing. Oh these green girls do they have reverence for anything except the fragility of their own pendulum of mood?

You but go to Rome and see the statue by Bernini to immediately understand that she's coming. There's no doubt about it. What is she getting off on?

— Jacques Lacan

Aren't I attractive? Aren't you attracted to me?

She is being manipulative and cruel, she knows. She who lets boys into her bed unthinkingly, as a consolation prize.

Why won't you just fuck me?

Ruth, Ruth. He stares into her eyes. Oh how they have hurt you Ruth.

She begs and pleads. She wrests his clothes away from him. He has a large penis flaring like a gray mushroom. A flesh tulip surrounded by a cloud of rust-colored hair. He lies there, skinny and vulnerable. She climbs on top of him. Begins to have sex with him. He lets her. He stares into her eyes helplessly. Then he begins to moan and moan and Ruth watches him writhe about. She watches him with curiosity.

Later he goes down on her, raising his wet face to stare into her eyes lovingly, his face glowing. She feels a shiver of revolt.

She did not desire to be loved and cherished and caressed. She desired a beast. Someone to destroy her. Her own Jack the Ripper. Her own serial killer. She did not want to make love.

She wanted to be fucked—over and over again repeating her own disappearance.

When they have sex now she thinks of HIM instead.

The first time we ever had sex you hurt me so badly that I was convinced my appendix had burst. You grabbed at me and shook me like a rag doll, throwing my legs over your shoulders, poking at my womb, my anus, my mouth. I had only known adoration before. Not this hate mixed with semen and want. I wrenched away from you like some hurt animal while you simmered in disgust, your penis dangling like a raw, red, piece of meat.

Afterwards Rhys kisses her tenderly. I love you Ruth. Ruth feels detached. Maybe that's why she did it. Because afterwards he is just someone else. Something happens and he is just like everybody else and then he can go. Then he can leave too.

Soon afterwards she began to be cold and distant. She began to complain that Rhys was being too clingy, that he bored her. And why couldn't he move out of his parents' house? And why couldn't he ever fuck her, really fuck her, just throw her against a wall and do vile things to her?

I can't do that, he would say sorrowfully to Ruth, like a dog that's been beaten. I'm in love with you. I love you too much.

To make sure it is really over Ruth knows what she has to do. She has to go and fuck someone else. She goes to Ava Gardner's leaving-do. A leaving-do, that's what they call a going-away party. She was going on an extended holiday to Egypt or somewhere similarly glamorous and remote and wouldn't be returning to Horrids.

At the pub Ruth spied a boy giving her the drunken eyes. She looked at him. He came over to talk to her. He was Canadian. He was studying here. Now he was studying her. He has touched her elbow twice. She cannot get over that almost detached curiosity of wondering what someone will look like, naked, suspended over her.

He was a filmmaker. That was what he is going to school for, anyway. I like film too she said. But then can't think of any film she had ever seen. He listed off directors—Cassavetes, Scorsese. She nodded and sipped her drink. She had never seen *Taxi Driver*. A cardinal sin. He grunted in astonishment, began to lecture her on its significance in film history, world history. Standing there in the crowded noisy pub, their beer splashing against their wrists, she decided that he was arrogant. She decided that she couldn't stand him. She decided that she will probably sleep with him anyway.

They go to his place. They sit on the couch. He is continuing the conversation. It is a one-way conversation. But later he will want it two-ways, and (if he's lucky) three.

And there is Ruth. See Ruth. She finds herself in situations, suddenly, on strange couches of strange men, pretending to listen.

He is still talking about himself. She is bored. He never asks about her. He puts on a record and starts talking about the band playing but she has never heard of them. He is dumbstruck. He begins to lecture her on the band's significance in music history, world history. She pretends to listen. She stares at her empty wineglass. She catches herself looming above her. She is her own ghost.

She has made herself very small on the scratchy sofa. It is that moment. She can feel it. He stops talking. He moves in towards her. His face scrapes against hers, leaving raised welts. His tongue tastes of beer and cigarettes. He is vaguely nauseating.

They go to his bedroom. He shows her something on his fancy Apple computer. He touches it longingly, with more care and feeling than he will later touch her. He shows her the film he has been making. He makes porn videos you can download on the Internet. Ruth stares at these girls, twisting and turning. They are green and ghostly. They writhe about on the floor. They do not know what to do. In those eyes, the sick of nerves or tranquilized boredom. Off-camera. A voice. That's right. Sexy. Ooh yeah baby. So so sexy.

Ruth looks about the bedroom. Is she being filmed? But she cannot locate any green flashing light.

And it begins. They begin to fool around. She is the fool. Her clothes fall off. His clothes fall off. Sometimes, gazing up at the ceiling tiles, hazy in her fog of consciousness, she thinks: Why? What am I doing this for? But she forgets and pretends to enjoy it. She makes all the appropriate moaning sounds. She digs her nails into his back, which he interprets as her being hot for him, more, more, when really she is steeling herself as he continues to pound away, while she looks at the green glow of the alarm clock, wondering how much time has elapsed.

It's getting out of control. I just wish I were a lot older or a lot younger.

— Jean Seberg in Otto Preminger's *Bonjour, Tristesse*

After the sale there was not much to do at work except try to look busy organizing cleaning wiping something whenever the horrible head appeared.

I see Ruth bored behind the counter, waiting for her shift to end. She reminds me of that painting by Degas, of the salesgirl at the hat shop. She is dressed in drab green, fingering one of the pastel dream creations, as if daydreaming of a life in which she would be the wearer.

Doors opening.
Mind the gap.

40p man had disappeared. Ruth hadn't seen him for an eternity. Had he picked a new walk to haunt?

She needed to go to Royal Mail to pick up a package her father had sent her. She walks up Brick Lane to Whitechapel, past the whine and drumbeat of Bollywood soundtracks, mixed with the hip hop emanating from cars. Past men in shawls and caps, who stand outside their storefronts, conversing with the rush. Women in veils silently processing down the street. Little children in knee socks run past. Past a large pack of pigeons pecking on the ground banging their heads against the ground looking looking for what?

Across the street, after the large mosque, is the massive London Royal Hospital. People here do not go to the hospital. They go to hospital, like it's a state of being. A warm day. Almost spring. Patients in robes and various states of undress, bruised arms pulling on their IV bags, sitting in their wheelchairs, on the steps, having a cigarette or talking on their mobile phones. Others, flanked by attendants in hospital scrubs, stand on the steps, staring into the street. She hands the attendant the slip through the hole in the glass. The attendant returns with an envelope. The postmark from Chicago. Ruth rips it open. It is money, in sterling. Enough to get by for the next few weeks. A belated Christmas present. No note.

She pushes through the Whitechapel markets. They are packing up for the day, sad pieces of fruit, a table of fake watches, cell-phone covers. Past a shop for school uniforms, disembodied plaid jumpers and navy blue shorts, a shop with saris on similarly headless mannequins, past a shop for dress dummies, arranged in sexual positions. She turns onto Brick Lane. It starts to rain softly, slippery on the cobblestones.

The men waiting outside her landlord's restaurant smile at her. They now know that she is not hungry. Or if she was hungry, that she would not dine there tonight. They recognize her by now. She wondered what they saw when they looked at her, head down, blonde bulb dirtying with the quickening rain.

She puts in her notice at Horrids. It is awkward running into Rhys all the time who stares at her like a wounded puppy. (They are both puppies, puppies I feel an urge to drown just to put them out of their misery. The euthanasia of youth.)

I feel sorry for you, Ruth. That's what he said when she told him about the Canadian.

Whatever. She said back.

When she goes to human resources to tell them of her plan she feels the most wonderful feeling. A bittersweet sense of transience hits her like a dizzy spell. She is merely a tourist. The end for her is the beginning. She would have many endings. They will be there forever. She would leave and leave and leave. And they would stay. This was their world, not hers.

Now that Ruth and Rhys are no longer an item, Agnes is inserted easily back into her life. They are best friends again for the time being, until they have another falling out. They are connected at the hip again, Siamese twins.

If I could smash that thing that houses me inside of myself…

— Angela of Foligno

Agnes had some Ecstasy. Ruth couldn't see a reason why not. To not be Ruth for a few hours. It was a favorite hobby for these girls, to escape their heads.

Deep breathe in. Exhale.

I'm so happy I'm so happy.

I don't remember ever being so happy.

Agnes is kneeling on the bed, rubbing her hands up and down her fleshy arms in a meditative motion. Her eyes fluttering back like an epileptic saint.

I can't stop smiling.
My cheeks hurt.

Ruth makes a snow angel in the mess of her clothes on the floor, humming to the movement of her arms.

Upanddown
Upanddown

She allows the warmth to spread throughout her body. Ummm ummm ummm she moans, feeling the vibration of her voice in her chest.

Hours spent in this rapturous state.

Let's check in on our drugged lovelies and see how they are faring.

The girls are both on the bed, facing each other, a mirror image. They have both stripped down to their underwear (it's so hot in here).

Can I feel your eyelashes.
Of course. Of course.
They're so soft. So soft.

They stroke each other's faces slicked with glitter. Golden. They stroke each other's lips, their baby fuzz. So beautiful. So. Soft. (Soft-core more like.)

Since Agnes is the more experienced drugmom, she makes sure dopey drugdaughter drinks some water. She pours a bottle onto Ruth's head. I baptize you. Mmm. Ruth's tongue strokes her teeth. Her skin too is now glistening.

Hey hey feel this

Agnes is running her wet hands over Ruth's arms, which makes them tingle all over.

Feelthis feelthis

Oh oh Ruth moans. Never had she felt such delight.

I look lovingly at all of their flaws they are too consumed to now notice. How their curly pubic hair peeks, pokes out from their panties. The hairs on their nipples they pluck when they remember. How cute their ripples of cellulite on their baby white thighs. Their map of freckles. The sagging curve of their bellies. The sweaty underside of their breasts. Their ribbons of stretch marks. How filthy the bottoms of their feet. The red bumps on their rough upper arms. How beautiful they see each other now, in their altered glow, how banal their surroundings. Yet how gorgeous I too find them, gorgeous and disgusting.

Ruth cannot speak her throat hurts she is chainsmoking menthols icy and delicious Agnes gives to her the indulgent mommy she is enjoying this my jaw hurts

Agnes and her play tongue hockey and licky-licky it is much more sweet and innocent than before it is sweet and innocent nothing sordid about their sweet kisses, their sweet love.

I love you
I love you too
I love you I love you

I love this
Don't end
Please don't end

A scratchy blanket is pulled over them in bed. They are innocent babies. Polymorphously perverse. Entranced by the textures of everything, is this her hair, is this my skin. They are outside of themselves. They have abandoned the premises. They have left the building.

Oh what wonderful phrases Ruth thinks. Oh what profound things she thinks too. She tries to tell Agnes but she cannot.

Agnes, Agnes.
What?
I forgot.

Oh, life, life, life. Life, life, life.

Agnes moans softly to herself. Hmmm. Hmmm. Hmmm.

Ruth was filled with such violence, such sublime joy. She is enflamed with tenderness. Her teeth chattering.

This can never end.
No, it can never end.
Please don't ever end.

Don't leave me Agnes.
I won't leave you Ruth.
Please don't ever leave.

They never wanted it to end never wanted it to end never wanted it to

— If I could dig a hole and hide from everyone, I'd do it.
— Do as elephants do, when they're unhappy, they just disappear.
— I don't know if I'm unhappy because I'm not free, or I'm not free because I'm unhappy.

— Jean-Luc Godard's *Breathless*

The next day. The depths of despair. Of dead and dread. All the joy has crept out of her body.

Ruth wakes up and it is evening. She has slept for what seems like days, slept like a leech stuck to her mattress.

Oh the noises, the fucking noises.

40% 50% 40% 50%

She reluctantly reemerges into the night, into the city with its cruel eyes. She is parched and craving sweet. She hasn't eaten all day. Nothing in the fridge of course.

Look (don't look)
Look (please don't look)

Her sunglasses mirror the reflection of the seething outside, closing in on her.

Her only reflection is her image.

Two Bengali kids, cigarettes hanging on their lips, loiter in the doorway of the newsagent. She lowers her eyes when she passes them, feeling them look her up and down, feeling the heat of their gaze. She buys chocolate, Sprite.

The kids harass her as she passes them again. You looking fine tonight lady. She ignores them. She attempts to turn into stone.

The noise has put her on edge. She is breaking down. She is Ingrid Bergman in *Gaslight.*

She walks tense among the terrible teem. She keeps on looking back, checking to see if anyone's following her. She makes eye contact with a few men who stop as she passes by.

She is a zombie. She is out of it. She walks down Brick Lane. She keeps pace behind two girls wearing silver stilettos, clinging to each other as they walk down the cobblestones. They look like they are supporting each other, like they can't walk without the other. She doesn't know where she's going. She passes by people drinking at candlelit tables, smoking on doorsteps, pouring out of gallery openings. More bodies, bodies, bodies. She feels fragile right now, exposed. *Salut, Ça va?*, a Frenchman waves at her from across the street. She ignores him too.

She passes alleys with the stench of piss. Past a dark street frequented by prostitutes. She feels the burn in her belly. She continues walking. Past the strip club. Past the big stone church. Past the tree like an armless woman howling in pain.

Hell is a city much like London—
A populous and a smoky city;
There are all sorts of people undone,
And there is little or no fun done;
Small justice shown, and still less pity.
— Percy Bysshe Shelley, "Peter Bell the Third" (Part the Third: Hell) quoted in Walter Benjamin's *The Arcades Project*

Without her schedule at Horrids she was set adrift. She now sleeps until the late afternoon, then lazes around, watching films, smoking, staring out the window. Finally she forces herself out one day, to head into central London, to walk around, think about finding another job (though temporary it will surely be). The streets are papered with junk, vomit, wrappers, flyers from the market.

She wishes she could clean herself of these dirty streets. She prays for the rain to wash it all away. She needs a flood pouring down absolution.

She hurries down the street, clutching her keys in her hand and her phone in the other, like protective talismans. The construction workers turn to consider her. She ducks her head and hustles past the jangle of rainbow-colored keys in a worker's hand, the other clasping a Styrofoam cup.

It is too much outside. The studies and the stares. She stumbles down the street, dry and shaky. Flashes in mirrored windows. She can't escape herself. Her face frantic, pink, smudged.

The mall next to Liverpool is made of green glass like the bottom of a pool flooded with light. It hurts her eyes.

They never stop following her. They all want something from her. They want a piece from her. They want her signature. They want her soul. It is a feeding frenzy. She is on all the cable stations. This just in: Ruth-gate.

They push push against her. It reaches a fever pitch. It is a crush. It is a circus. It is too much pressure. Leave me alone! She wants to beg. She hides behind sunglasses and hats and phony disguises. She is a train wreck. We gape at her. (Why don't we try to save her?)

Breaking news–Ruth breaks down!

Waiting at the crosswalk, she thinks, what's that thing that keeps drivers filling with rage throbbing with impatience from lifting the brake and plowing through a pedestrian? What keeps them from swallowing that brief impulse of glee, like stomping on a robin skittering past on the sidewalk?

(I want to stomp on their fragile stalks not yet formed, those spiky buds creeping up through moist dirt.)

Today she doesn't want to live in her skin.
Sheneededwantedneeded to peel it off, just peel it off.

She tries to look for work on the high streets. The constant refrain: Do you have a CV? Just leave your CV. Your CV, your CV. Your proof of identity. She is having an identity crisis. Who am I? (Is that me?) Who do I want to become? She journeys invisible through fog. She has no memory of herself. Surrounded by the gray, the gray, the gray. She passes out herself laid flat on a piece of paper, mumbling thanks to willing hands.

A realization—everyone in central London is a tourist. You can tell by the uncertainty in their eyes. But Ruth is used to being a tourist. Being a girl is like always being a tourist, always conscious of yourself, always seeing yourself as if from the outside.

She waits and waits for the call, any call, and goes home at dark, following the exodus of the properly employed. Tottenham Court Road. Holborn. Change here for the Piccadilly.

Doors closing. Mind the gap.

Chancery Lane. St. Paul's. Bank. Liverpool.

She sits at Soho Square, watching the pigeons. The fragile yellow pom-poms from the trees fall on her coat, in her hair. Pigeon beasts who look dyed in ink dart about skeptically. The red warty prong of pigeon toes. Amber glass dots for eyes. Metallic purple and green necklaces. There is a king pigeon with white tuft and turkey chin, cooing. They rapidly disperse at the faintest sign of crumb or wrapper, like a massive breeze through the trees. The weakest of the pack fly back disappointed. A little girl dives through the pigeons. A Godzilla baby.

A Japanese couple think they're playing heroics by emptying out the contents of their plastic bag. The pigeons form a desperate orgy, jumping onto each other, while those on the fringe dart about excluded from the frenzy.

Ruth listens to construction workers talk swollenly in foreign tongues. The little girl chases after a freak white bird, an albino pigeon.

In the center of the square a statue with a pecked-out face. Charles, says the plaque. It is Charles, in sandstone armory, Charles in the age of powdered wigs of curling hair. A dappled pigeon sits on his head like a crown. Hand tossed on waist, the other wrist aristocratically positioned. Face pecked away.

The desperate monsters purr. It is once again feeding time. A man on the bench across from her in the circle throws some bread from an uneaten baguette. Word has gotten out and almost instantly a flock lands in front of their crumb king, hoping, praying, for some bread. A fruitless exodus. The amount tossed only satisfies a few pecks. The rest mill about on the checkerboard concrete stupidly. They are still setting up camp, hoping for the same benevolent gesture. A few loners strike out until they fly over Ruth's head, spotting a messy crisp-eater. Then again, and again. They are exhausting. A yellow pom-pom sticks to her stockings.

She hears the lulling tambourine approach. Four Hare Krishnas appear, meandering hopefully through the park. The thromp, thromp of the drum. Gym shoes. Flowing melon-colored saris. Heads wrapped in scarves. Dirt-colored hooded sweatshirts. One just in jeans and Nikes. They beat methodically their orange bongo and bells. They sing in unison their hopeful tune, palms upturned.

They are a constant presence in the square, her Hare Krishnas, her saviors, scaring the pigeons away.

Ruth heads up Tottenham Court Road to look for movie times. She sees films on her day off, though every day is now a day off. She goes to the movies often, to fill in the space of the day, although she knows she needs to conserve her dwindling pile of pounds. This is her other sacred space. The calm privacy of the movie theater, surrounded by shadowy strangers.

She pushes into a rush-hour train home, stuck between the armpits of businessmen, briefcases, beery breath. Gossiping about a colleague. She tries to follow:

He slagged him off.
He's an all right sort.

Tottenham Court Road. Holborn. Change here for the Piccadilly.

Chancery Lane. St. Paul's. Bank. Liverpool.

Can you please spare 40p?
40p man is back. He has returned.

I would go out tonight
But I haven't got a stitch to wear

— The Smiths, "This Charming Man"

Agnes wants Ruth to go with her to a party near Old Street. It is a dress-up party. The theme is circus. Agnes loves to play dress up. Last costume party they were Catherine Deneuve and Françoise Dorléac, Deneuve's real-life sister, from *The Young Girls of Rochefort.* Ruth was the Deneuvian blonde, Agnes was the redhead who gets Gene Kelly, who died in a car crash in real life.

Today Agnes dresses up like an old-fashioned tightrope walker, like out of Toulouse-Lautrec. She wears a top hat over her orange ringlets and a red leotard over webbed red tights. Red boots, of course. Her leotard is so tight her breasts bulge out and her crotch looks painted on, like an unsexed doll. Completing the outfit is her cigarette holder and black gloves up to her elbows. She has spent a week planning her outfit. Ruth doesn't know what to wear so Agnes lets her borrow her plastic sunglasses in the shape of stars and she wears one of Agnes's dresses with one of her feather boas wrapped around her neck. That is her costume. She is in disguise. She is Agnes for the night.

Walking outside past the ogle of men standing outside the strip club across from the gas station, past the tree like an armless woman howling in pain, past the big stone church.

The party is at a large warehouse. In the back Agnes and Ruth pass back and forth a bottle of vodka. They roll their eyes at girls teetering on high heels as if on stilts. There is a catwalk erected. There is going to be a fashion show. One model sets herself on fire at the end of the catwalk, to the roar of the crowd. She is then swallowed up in a blanket and extinguished as two men carry her backstage.

Agnes sees someone she knows and leaves Ruth alone, pressing up against the wall. Agnes always a lightning bug agitating against the glass jar, always somewhere better to go. Alone Ruth feels like a little girl who has invaded her mother's closet.

Why are you here? The man next to her is well-tailored and groomed, wearing a designer suit over a white T-shirt with no tie. Ruth had been aware that he was eavesdropping on her and Agnes's banter, and she even caught him scribbling a few words on a pad of paper he kept in his pocket. He looked like a painter, Ruth thought. Some sort of artist. He was the same height as Ruth. He had an impish quality to him, and a handsome, clean-shaven face.

Why am I here? Ruth repeats. She is warm and tingly from the vodka. She is not wasted but with a little effort she could soon be. (Oh, our wasted youth.)

Yes. The man takes out a pack of Gauloises, offers Ruth one. She accepts. The cigarette tickles the back of her throat. Who do you know here? He is not unfriendly. He is curious. Green girls are used to the attention of strange men.

Oh, my friend invited me.

The redhead? he asks. He has a sinister look about his face, but it is pleasantly sinister, like Buster Keaton.

Ruth nods.

She's the Big Bad Wolf, isn't she? he mock-whispers in her ear.

Who, Agnes? Ruth smiles in her small way.

The man puffs on his cigarette elegantly. He shrugs. Whatever her name is.

Does that make me Little Red Riding Hood?

He appraises her. You're not Gramma, darling.

Ruth feels comfortable joking with him. How do I know you're not the Big Bad Wolf?

His eyes glimmer. He is obviously charmed. I could be.

I'm Ruth. She offers impetuously.

He gives her his hand as if on a silver tray. Delighted Ruth. Teddy.

Teddy. She repeats to remember.

Ruth. Like Keats's poem. Are you sick for home, baby Ruth?

Home? She considers for a moment. I don't know. I mean, what is home?

This amuses Teddy greatly. Aah, I see. You are like the poem. Like Ruth in the Bible. Are you wandering, Ruth? Are you peri-pat-etic? He is teasing her, but she does not mind.

I don't know what that means. I'm a bit pathetic, however.

But what are you trying to find, Madame Pathos?

She smiles.

I like your hair. Quite Edie Sedgwick.

Ruth pats her head nervously. It's growing out. Thank you. She demurs.

Just then Agnes appears at her elbow. Can we go? She simmers impatiently, shooting daggers at Teddy, who seems amused by her animosity. Ruth nods dutifully at Agnes her master, what a bossy girl, but tries to have an apologetic expression at Teddy.

So can I see you again, my nightingale? Teddy asks.

Why not? Ruth sing-songs her mobile number to him, as he's tapping it into his phone, the last digit just in time as Agnes pulls her away.

That guy is BIZ-arre, a hungry Agnes scowls as they stand in the queue for the 24-hour bagel shop on Brick Lane.

I liked him. Ruth felt this, but her feelings on the matter could melt from another's hostility, she wasn't sure.

He gives me the creeps. I've seen him before. I think he's a poof.

A what?

A poof. Agnes made an indecipherable gesture. You know. Gay.

Ruth shrugs. Agnes was just trying to be a jerk, Ruth thinks. Upset that Teddy found Ruth more interesting. Why would I care? In her mind that was better. That would mean she didn't have to sleep with him.

Will you go with me to the clinic Monday? They are eating the warm dough wrapped in wax paper while walking through the nocturnal haze of Brick Lane, the puddles reflective in the street.

Why?

Because...*Ruth.* Agnes can always say Ruth's name like it is an insult. I have to get something *done.* She emphasizes the final word in a huff.

Ruth's heart thuds. Is it Olly's? She doesn't know why she is asking this.

Ruth...Agnes sighs heavily, tossing her half-eaten bagel in the nearest bin. I don't want to talk about it.

Okay. Ruth tries to think of something to make Agnes smile. I'll buy you an ice-cream cone afterwards.

Agnes smiles weakly. Okay.

The two girls link arms, walking home, their costumes suddenly ridiculous in the hangover of early morning.

I live my part too—only I can't figure out what my part is in this movie.

— Edie Sedgwick in Andy Warhol's *Kitchen*

Agnes smokes cigarettes for breakfast, watching the blankness of the street outside the window. Human ants scurry across occasionally. Agnes doesn't look at them. She looks beyond them. She is wearing red high heels that have scraped off white flakes of paint on the windowsill and a red bandana that pulls her red hair off her face. She isn't wearing any makeup. She looks paler, her own shadow.

Ruth eats Green and Black's chocolate ice-cream with a fork. The flatmates don't talk. They listen to music. Nico's "Femme Fatale" fills the room with melancholy. Agnes smokes and Ruth tiptoes around her, watchfully. Mindfully. Agnes is in trouble, she thinks. That's the old-fashioned way of putting it. She's in trouble. She feels very important somehow. She has never taken a friend to get an abortion. A friend in her condition. That's what they say. In your condition. What is the condition, exactly? If then, then what? Well, they all now knew the if then. Ruth was still unsure about the then what. Ruth thinks back to that night and imagines that their coupling on the bed with Olly was the sordid conception. And in a way, bizarre as it sounds, that the baby was hers as well.

Agnes is late for her appointment. She is quickly beckoned by a white coat and clipboard. Ruth sits on a hardback chair and pretends not to stare at the women occupying chairs around her. Each one to their own chair, their own private thoughts. There is a heavy mood to the waiting room. They are all women from the neighborhood. Faces of ripe fruit, wrinkled raisins. Most of them are veiled and dressed in long robes. Bengali she guesses. Muslim most likely. Ruth does not know exactly. If she had to point at a map she would probably put Bangladesh between India and Pakistan. (It isn't.) There was some kind of war, which is always, of course, terrible, that is all she knows. It's not like she has time to read the newspaper.

A woman in a burqa sits across from her. She is covered except for her hands. She has heard of burqas on the news. The First Lady begging the camera to free these women of their coverings so itchy and so hot. Ruth wonders what it would be like to hide away from all of the staring eyes of the street. She thinks that she would like to wear a veil. Or maybe just a glamorous black headscarf, like Jackie Kennedy. She imagines herself in the part of mourning widow, following her husband's coffin while being followed by the TV. On the woman's lap an expensive leather handbag is perched. Ruth looks around the room. On all of the laps rest various leather handbags in competition pradas guccis marc jacobs. One woman reaches down and scratches an ankle. Little children in shorts and colorful tees play on their mother mountains. Occasionally they are admonished in thick tongues but mostly they are allowed to roam, to flirt with other strangers in the room. Ruth smiles at a boy with a map stain on his forehead. He pretends to play shy, hiding behind his mother mountain. She looks away, already bored with the game, perhaps nervous the mother will chide him disapprovingly.

A man sits several seats down from the burqa woman with the prada handbag. She wonders whether he's her husband. She has seen families strolling slowly down Brick Lane. The older women stroll behind. Ruth looks at the little playful girls and wonders if as their bodies lengthen they will be wrapped in garbs of solemnity.

After a while, Ruth's mind is absolutely devoid of thoughts. It must be the sugar, the tension in the room. She is struck with this impression of not really being there, in the waiting room. Ruth's mother would tell her that when she was a little baby she could just sit in her stroller for hours, regarding the world with her soft gray eyes. She just stared and stared, regarding the towering populace with an element of remove, even then.

Ruth was now doubled over onto the chair, as if praying. Stomach cramps. Trapped gas, they called it here. All she had consumed all day was smoke, heavy feelings, and chocolate ice cream. All she had left was a hole inside. All she had left was a searing ache.

Ruth watches a solemn procession of veiled women walk up the stairs, advancing slowly towards the front counter. Each woman takes a bag of condoms from the receptionist at the front desk and proceeds back down the stairs. The package quickly disappears underneath the black hollow of their sleeve. She feels she is somehow witnessing a delicate ritual between Brick Lane wives, that she is not supposed to be there during this silent parade. It seems since she's got to London she's always stumbling upon rituals beyond her comprehension.

Finally Agnes walks out.

How are things? Ruth asks.

Agnes pats her stomach. Flat. She is parroting Julie Christie in *Darling.* Ruth knows this, of course.

Do you feel okay?

Agnes shrugs. She takes out her compact from her purse and applies lipstick, streaks of red around and around the track fiercely.

They say I might have some discomfort but otherwise good as new.

Agnes appraises herself from each angle. She says hello to herself her old self. Puff puff puff the shine away from her nose, flick flick the red off her front teeth, and then a satisfied snap shut. She slips her compact back into her purse. She looks around the waiting room. Ugh. Let's get out of here.

Agnes does not want to go immediately home. So they take the train and get ice cream cones from a Cadbury cart and walk around near Leicester Square, around the Mall. To an outside observer they are two girls light as air enjoying the first signs of spring.

Agnes is silent for a long while. Then she suddenly begins talking, to the sky, to the buildings, to the cars. Talking, talking, talking. Not to Ruth. Almost to herself. Ruth tries to listen, although she feels awkward seeing this different side of Agnes, Agnes without the armor.

Finally, Agnes speaks. It was horrible. Horrible.

The—procedure? asks Ruth, trying to be delicate.

No, no. She pauses. All of it. I felt so—violated. Like some horrible creature had invaded my body. I needed to get it out. I would have reached inside and torn it out if I could. My body threatening to distort beyond all recognition. She shudders, and looks with distaste at her ice cream cone, as if startled to find it in her hand. Wordlessly, she hands it over to Ruth, who alternates licks with each hand.

Agnes is silent for a long while. They walk over to a park where they can sit on a bench and watch the ducks. Ruth wonders whether it's a painful sight to see momma duck trailing her little bits of fuzz. Agnes lights a cigarette and sits there smoking at the ducks. When she is done with her cigarette she throws it into the water, lights another one. Finally, she continues her private monologue.

Imagine—my body becoming some public domain. Waddling around like some gross aberration. People feeling they can touch my stomach. People giving up their seats to me on the bus. It's like, fuck off. I don't want that.

Does the father know? asks Ruth. She realizes this is a stupid thing to say.

Agnes does not respond. There was no father, she says, finally, almost dreamily.

You mean, that…

Now sharply, as if she had woken up. There. Was. No. Father. She turns towards Ruth. All right? She rolls her eyes. Jeezus, Ruth.

Ruth doesn't say anything. A frozen moment between them. Agnes often had a way of making Ruth feel small. She flicks at the little hard bump under her fingernail. Agnes smokes as if angry. Is she mad at me? Ruth wonders.

Finally Agnes speaks. I felt like I was walking around with a big scarlet letter P on me. P for pathetic.

How about KU for knocked up? Ruth is anxious to make Agnes laugh, to break this mood.

Agnes does laugh, relentingly. W/C. With child.

There's multiple meanings to that, Ruth quips.

That's what I felt like. I felt like someone had taken a giant shit inside me.

They sit for a while again in a more companionable silence and stare off into nothingness, each to her own thoughts.

Agnes starts talking about a film she saw the other day. Talking. Talking. Talking. Running of the mouth. Have you seen Have you seen Have you seen. Ruth lets her talk. And then And then And then. Lets her film synopsis bathe over her as she watches the ducks. Two men with dark sunglasses are watching them. She can feel them watching her and Agnes, admiring their attractiveness. She can sense they are talking about them, wondering whether they should come over, wondering which one they want, weighing their chances, their choices. She hopes they won't come over. She wonders if Agnes sees them too. If this is who she is performing for, her always audience.

The operatic sigh. The animated gestures. The smoke was even part of Agnes's act, pirouetting up and up into the air.

Was it the infinite sadness of her eyes that drew him or the mirror of himself that he found in the gorgeous clarity of her mind?

— F. Scott Fitzgerald, *This Side of Paradise*

She began to see Teddy regularly.

He took her to dinner. He always paid. He took her shopping at Liberty. He bought her a little black dress there. It was not even on sale.

She enjoyed trying it on for him twirling around outside of the dressing room. Well, you should definitely have that, he said. You need it. Of course. I see that.

The shopgirls seemed more respectful of her as they carefully wrapped the dress up in the black tissue paper, and laid it gently into the deep purple bag.

This is too generous of you she gushed.
It's nothing he shrugged.

He was so curious about her, her life, her thoughts. She didn't know what to make of his attention. She didn't know whether he was wooing her, whether she was supposed to eventually go to bed with him. She didn't know if he thought of her in that way. He treated her like a child, like a delicate flower. He called her *ma petite poupée, ma petite fille.* She found his pretension, his ostentation, somewhat charming, even if he was too intense at times. (Ugh, I cannot believe she doesn't see through this.)

At bookshops together on Charing Cross Road. She stared longingly at the fiction shelves. He bought her the books he thought she should read, which were mostly the obvious books, because he wasn't that well-read either, but liked to see himself as her brilliant tutor. (Doesn't every green girl need a Svengali, trading her charm for his experience?)

He was always scribbling something down in her presence. He wrote for various magazines, although he said he was working on a novel (they always are).

I write too she said. Or I'd like to.

I'd love to read some of your material he said, knowing she doesn't have any material besides herself, which is still potentially more interesting than anything he will ever have. She was a rough draft. She was impressionable, everyone left their impressions on her. To be a writer she would have to take herself back as a character. She would have to escape from her life as muse. Escape from her role as the blank slate, which everyone scribbled on.

Yes he is writing a novel. She is the novel. It is the book of his Ruth, the book of her youth. He freely takes pages.

If she had looked at the open page of his notebook she would have seen these notations:

—she has a young girl's mannerism of asking constant approval with every comment

—as ethereal as the Holy Ghost

But for now she was happy being a character. She was happy having dinners and dresses bought for her. She was happy to have someone to walk the streets with, ride the tube with. There were fewer stares.

He takes his delectable American gamine to the Queen's Gardens to walk amidst the roses and watch the black swans curl into each other. (He writes: She is at home among the slender budding stems. She has a charming habit of biting her lower lip while deep in thought.)

He lectures her on not only the literature she should read, but films she should see, philosophy she should know. He lectures her about the war. She takes on his opinions. She is malleable. She is his raw material. His Galatea. A fistful of clay, gray gray gray. Afterward he puts her on a pedestal.

He takes her to see the Francis Bacons at the Tate Britain. (He writes: Her teeth are childishly arranged in her mouth.)

She stands in front of a triptych silently, considering, as if at some sort of church, while Teddy watches her. Her facial expression difficult to detect.

Three gruesome distorted bodies set against a rage-filled orange. The open mouth. What is there to do but scream? And no sound comes out. We have lost ourselves. We offer ourselves up to the popes of abandon, of frenzied despair. Our identities gone. Our faces blurred, racing.

She was overjoyed looking at them, at those faces that swirled and swirled, but when he pressed her to explain further she couldn't. He always wanted to know her thoughts, what she was thinking. It's horrible and beautiful, she says. Like life, horrible and beautiful. She is trying to be deep. Or maybe she is accidentally profound. Then she shivers, suddenly. (He writes: She looks far away for a moment, far far away, so far away I could never reach her.)

He takes his Ophelia to a production of *Hamlet* in Covent Garden. He is trying to cultivate her. As they get up to leave he finds that she has scribbled on her program that she leaves on her seat. It reads:

To die, to sleep, then nothing more? Nothing, nothing more?

He silently pockets this find. He takes out his notebook and writes:

She drowns herself in her own reflections.

I believe in the flapper as an artist in her particular field, the art of being—being young, being lovely, being an object…

— Zelda Fitzgerald

He takes her to a party. It is an adult party at an adult home with expensive, adult things. Ruth wears her new dress. She is happy to go to be looked at but she is shivering in it because it is cold inside. Ruth feels underdressed. All the women have fancy shawls and fancy jewelry and she just has the fancy dress. She stumbles around, outside of herself, looking at all of the well-dressed women looking her up and down.

Teddy presents her to the hostess. She is a sculptor, he tells Ruth. Her husband is a painter.

Your home is lovely. Ruth says shyly.

The woman also looks Ruth up and down. She smiles, coldly, politely. Well isn't she lovely. She says to Teddy, as if Ruth isn't even there. (I hate her too, I am annoyed on Ruth's behalf.) Always nice to meet one of Teddy's friends, she says. As if there have been many others. She seems to have heard of Ruth before their introduction. The most important part of an introduction always occurs in one's absence. Ruth's role is just to stand there.

And what do you do? The dreaded question.

Nothing. Ruth says. She is uncomfortable. The green girl does not like to be out of her element. She does not like to leave her comfort zone. All of a sudden Ruth feels silly in her new dress and her glistened pout. She feels young and awkward and naked to the world. But inside deeper inside she is furious and decides she hates this woman and wants to leave immediately.

Can we leave now? She begs. No, not yet. Teddy is annoyed, impatient. So she follows Teddy around dumbly.

They are in a circle of people. They are talking about an exhibition at the White Cube. They ignore her as if she isn't there. So she doesn't try to contribute anything. She grows meek and then melancholic.

Ruth sits down on a couch and decides to feel very sorry for herself. She decides she is going to drink as much as possible to drown her miseries.

What is wrong with you? Teddy is standing over her. I want to go home. She has now reverted to being an eight-year-old. She is close to throwing a drunken teary tantrum. She finally collapses into herself.

Fine, fine, I'll take you home. He sighs heavily, a disappointed father. On the train home he berates her: Why are you like this? Why do you act like this?

But Ruth has already turned off from him. The green girl shrinks when someone tries to pry underneath. She begins to pout if pried too far.

She decides not to see Teddy anymore. And that is that. The green girl draws decisive lines in the sand. The green girl breaks easily with her past.

She knows now she has to get a job. Just another job where she will be just another salesgirl. Another disposable job, another disposable boy, her disposable existence.

I can't explain myself, I'm afraid, Sir, because I'm not myself you see.

— Alice in Lewis Carroll's *Alice in Wonderland*

Would you consider yourself a leader? Ruth is being interviewed for a position at a high street women's clothing store at Oxford Circus. Her interrogator is a tiny blonde girl named Alice, utterly proper, immaculately groomed. Alice is outfitted in standard flower child regalia, wearing a flimsy peasant top that revealed a dainty patch of freckled white and a thick leather belt fitted over narrow hips, the kind Ruth had seen everywhere in London, even given away free in some women's magazines.

Ruth doesn't know what being a leader has to do with folding shirts, but she has rent to pay so she answers what she is supposed to. So she answers Yes.

Okay. Soft, careful voice. Alice marks something on her clipboard using a gold glitter pen. They are going down a list of questions. Ruth has had enough jobs to know how to stay inside the right box.

Okay, Ruth, what makes you want to be in sales? With that the blonde girl looks up, with her patient tiny heart-shaped face. There was something about this girl—and there were legions of them in London—English roses so unflawed in their femininity, so petite and prim, so perfectly contained, that made Ruth feel like something was threatening to spill out of her when she was around them, an avalanche of American vulgarity. She felt her armpits a damper black.

Well…

Ruth's eyes wander around the cramped office surroundings, settling on the headlines of yesterday's *Metro*. MAN BEHEADED ON STREET, it read.

I like to shop so…

Charles and Camilla at some social function. Camilla wearing a hat like a well-behaved blue chicken roosting on her head. Smiling, arms around each other. They looked happy. They were her parents' age, maybe older. Happy. She had seen pictures like that, pictures where her parents were at some wedding, poised standing behind a table. Happy.

Alice's eyes loom large and blue at her. Waiting. I don't want to be in sales, actually Ruth thinks. I hate selling anything. I'm not made for the rejection. That telemarketing job for the Chicago Symphony. Hi, Mr. So-and-So…Click. Good evening, Mrs. So-and-so…Click.

I like to shop so I feel that I've really, like, cracked that thing that makes women or girls or whatever, buy. She has no idea what she's saying. Her palms start to sweat.

The managerial Alice nods. She is so serious, so English. Pursing her pink pout gently glossed. Check. She puts the clipboard down. Crosses her legs the other way. Gold ballet slippers. Skinny ankles.

Well let me tell you a bit about our philosophy.... She launches into a well-worn monologue about the mythical customer, their needs, their wants, studying her hands clasped in front of her. Ruth studies them as well. Her hands soft skin ivory white, tiny little bones, like two fragile doves. They look cold. Ruth fights the urge to fold her warm sweaty hands over them, to feel their pulse.

I was exhausted by all I'd been through my—nerves broke. I was on the verge of—lunacy almost!

— Vivien Leigh as Blanche DuBois in Elia Kazan's *A Streetcar Named Desire*

At night she lies in her soft tomb, listening to the constant soundtrack outside, of angry cars pulling up and speeding away, slamming doors, loud sometimes charged conversations in other tongues, the cackle of callers shouting gossip to each other across the street, the clomp of heels and cowboy boots, the sloppy antics of drunken American and English groups.

Ruth felt like she was always moving, fleeing from some scene of a crime. The impermanence of her life was starting to weigh on her. The constant move from place to place. Where will she stop? Nobody knows. She was in permanent exile. She was serving her sentence. One dingy darkened room to another. Furry monsters hiding under the bed, ghosts of dust evading the lazy non-broom. The world was pregnant with noises. The humping of the Spaniards downstairs. Dogs moaning. The late-night orgy on the streets. 50% off! 40%! 50%!

The noises oh the noise. The noise makes one forget oneself. The noise so thick it can tear away at one's identity. The foam earplugs stuffed into her skull could not drive out the orchestra of the night. She curled shut, trying to drown out the blanket of horns and screams stretched over her head like a leather canvas, ballooned and pulled until there was a cloud of cacophony in her head. Car noises, the honks, the squealing brakes, the sliding by on the wet street. The Bollywood soundtracks issuing forth from the windows.

Agnes was never home anymore at night. All she would say is she was on a date with a gentleman. The same gentleman? Ruth would ask. No, a different one. They take me places, is what she would say. Men. That's the ticket. Those boys, I never went anywhere. Ruth didn't know exactly where Agnes was trying to go. She had entirely different clothes now, one of the rich men Agnes was seeing, a stockbroker, had let her run up his credit card at Selfridges. A flurry of expensive labels. She had quit her job at the coffee shop as well. Looks like I might be looking for a place by myself now, she had said coyly to Ruth. Something more central, you know. Something more comfortable.

Last time she saw her Agnes had bleached her hair blonde. Ruth looked up from her soft tomb. What do you think? Agnes asked. I was going for Dietrich in *Scarlet Empress.* I was thinking more Harlow, *Dinner at Eight,* said Ruth. Aah, I like that. There was something unhinged about Agnes lately. She would run in frantically, unzip herself out of her evening dress, cursing all the while, hopping into a sequined number. She had taken to lining her eyes thick and black. But Ruth understood it too. It felt like the appropriate response to this city. Lately everything seemed to be going outside the lines. Maybe it was the spring. Maybe everything seemed crazed.

I had the job for three weeks. It was dreary. You couldn't read; they didn't like it. It would feel as if I were drugged, sitting there, watching those damned dolls, thinking what a success they would have made of their lives if they had been women. Satin skin, silk hair, velvet eyes, sawdust heart—all complete.

— Jean Rhys, *Good Morning, Midnight*

Inside the massive white two-story light box Ruth can only see what is directly in front of her, watching blurry packs of cooing girls lifted up and down the elevator. All around her so much color. Spring was here, signs announced, coral and sky blue and mint-green. Ruth looks at the outfit arranged on a mannequin, a haphazard bag-lady chic, layered with strands and strands of beads. Ruth saw countless girls in her neighborhood wearing the same type of ensemble. Should I dress like that? she thinks. Maybe I should dress like that.

She staggers through her tour, she and another girl, following their managerial nymph, who was wearing a lacy eggplant camisole topped off by a black knit shrug, with camouflage shorts and a mess of gold chains coasting between sharp collarbones. The other new girl had thick thighs covered in rainbow tights, she wore a short ripped jean skirt, black Converse all-stars, and a black hooded sweatshirt. From the neck up she styled herself like Bettie Page with a ponytail, shiny onyx bangs framing a pale, made-up mask of scarlet lips and bright-blue lids. Her face was covered with a sheen of sweat. Ruth could hear her breathing as Alice chatted away.

They tromp after the slipping trajectory of Alice's ballet flats as she walks around with a clipboard introducing them to the clothes, all anointed with girl's names. Ruth tries to make mental notes. But the store music floods and fills and thickens her brain until she can't think. And the other girl keeps on breathing heavily next to her. Name was Vienna. Face shiny like a Sacher torte.

Hello, Veronica trousers (don't say pants) in tan or black.

Hello, Monica cords, in slate-gray or cream or burnt orange.

Hello Amanda ribbed tanks, in every color.

Hello, Kimmy Tees, Stella camisoles, Sophie military fatigues (which Alice was wearing), Katie shorts, Lynn peasant blouse.

Say hello, girls.

Hello, girls.

Alice shows them how to fold a Lynn peasant blouse using a plastic board, just go there and there and flip and there you go. Ruth and the other girl stand there and watch. The other girl emits a strange, sour scent.

Now you try it, Alice steps away.

Heart beating, Ruth tries to fold the blouse with the board. Her fold comes apart as soon as she slips the board out. Vienna manages to manipulate the blouse into a perfect square. Sorry, Ruth whispers. Alice waves her white hand, bangles a reassuring jingle. It'll come to you, she promises.

Waiting in the station going home she sits next to a woman whose bag of crisps peek out from her purse. Ruth's stomach grumbles. She fights the urge to snatch a crisp away.

Across from her on the train is a young girl with a blank beautiful face. Her hair done up in an updo, brown hair swept across forehead then pinned back. She wears eyeliner that springs up from the corner of her eyes like tiny alarmed cat claws. A mess of black string, in which are buried several sandwich crumbs, makes up a scarf wrapped around her shoulders and neck. She wears the prerequisite black boots tucked in painted-on dark jeans. Ruth recognizes the scarf from the store. When she stands up and jumps over the gap at the Liverpool stop, she reveals two little buttocks like a perfectly outlined heart. She pulls down her top with a self-conscious gesture, tapping away.

Up the escalator, deep down below, as if from the bowels of hell, Ruth watches a pair of girls go down the other way, wearing identical plastic sunglasses in the shape of stars.

With a half shriek of joy the old man forced a passage within, resumed at once his original bearing, and stalked backward and forward, without apparent object, among the throng.

— Edgar Allan Poe, "The Man of the Crowd"

Today is her first day of work. She will be tested, tried out. She will be tested to see if she "fits into the family," Alice said.

She is thrown into the crush of Saturday. Mobs and mobs of assaulting femininity. A rhythm starts to build amidst all the chaos. Stagger around, pick up errant clothes, greet newcomers. Do you work here? Do you work here? Fold, fold, greet, greet. Do you work here? Do you work here? Point to your badge. Nod yes. Do you have this in another size? A different color? Nod yes, yes. Remember to smile. (Always.) Keep on moving. Set to a soundtrack of numbing piped-in music, bouncing while Ruth staggers around.

The work is hellish. Piles and piles of clothes like deflated corpses. A Sisyphean task. Take a piece from the pile, insert it on a hanger, or fold it neatly, use the board. Put it away, come back, the pile grows. Scoop up trashy translucent innards from the fitting rooms. Walk out with a body of clothes, heavy, back breaking. Fold and fold and fold.

Clang of the door. Armies of heads swivel. A new one. Always a new one. They pour in, they leave, more come. Guarded over by a team of Jamaican security guards doing systematic searches of plastic bags, This way ma'am, Can you come here ma'am, you need to be detagged. She hears them speaking to each other in a mysterious language. She locks eyes with one, tight dreadlocks, large white teeth, skinny frame lost in a billowing blue uniform shirt. He grins at her. She tries to smile back but she is zonked. After an hour of this she is already watching the clock.

How's it going? He asks.
Okay? Is it always like this? (What she wants to say: This is a fucking nightmare. I'm losing my mind.)
Knowing smile, nod, the policeman stance, hands clasped in back, rocking forward.
Saturdays. He says.

She folds and folds and the piles keep springing up. An ensemble of girls playing pick-up, The Danaids of Oxford Street, carrying water in leaky jars from the river's edge, filling and refilling, folding and refolding. Doomed to repeat their task, over and over.

Her break. Finally. A breath. She finds the employee room. Smells of other people's reheated food. Popcorn billowing in the microwave. She sits on a hardback chair, trying not to smell the jacket potato the girl next to her is eating out of tin foil. Al-u-min-ium, remember, not a-lu-minum. Everyone straining necks watching *Friends* on the small TV perched above. Tapes of the television show lined up next to the VCR. Seemingly every season. She sits and watches with them. She's seen this episode before. She laughs as well. Tears spring to her eyes. She is happy to hear familiar voices.

Another episode playing. Everyone else claps along with the opening credits.

I have a question for you, says one girl, her potato under siege in front of her.

What?

Why do you wear all black? The other girls at the table, previously involved with the show or their tabloid magazines or texting boyfriends on their mobiles, now look towards her. So suspicious, scrutinizing. Cast thy nighted color off.

I don't know. Ruth examines a smudged Page Three Girl opened up on the table. I wear color sometimes.

Jacket Potato Girl persists. You've been here twice already, and you've worn black every time.

Ruth looks down at herself. She had used her employee discount to purchase a tank top from the store just for that day, and it was not black, it was a dark gray Amanda. She looked at her sad black bra, the straps showing, digging in red brutal marks in her shoulders. But she doesn't have any energy to debate the point. She looks up at the television. She feels like a shock, as if she has been slapped. Pink. (Perhaps someone does need to get a thicker skin.)

I don't know. I guess I don't own that many clothes, still looking up at the TV, as if studying it. Phoebe is playing her guitar, long blonde ponytail swinging. Her voice rings out defensive. All of a sudden Ruth hated Jacket Potato Girl. She hated all of them. She was never coming back. She just had to get through the day.

Navigating the mob. Her security guard laughs at her frantic expression whenever she scurries by him near the front entrance, arms full of battered clothes, looking like she's going to run to freedom. Knowing if she came too close she'd set off a medley of warning sounds.

First day.

Can you tell.

He nods his head. Yup.

She sees Alice's blonde head bobbing towards her in the crowd.

Are you married.

No why would I be married. I'm young.

White teeth. You're not that young.

No, I'm not, she sighs to herself. I'm not this young. I'm not this young. Not anymore.

Alice reaches her through the crowd. Faces and faces. Ruth, I need you. She bows her head, meek, suppliant. Waves goodbye to her security guard, a wink of two fingers. Sent on a reconnaissance mission in the fitting rooms.

End of her shift. How did I do? A little girl, still wanting to please. Fine, fine, said Alice. We'll give you a call.

The end is near! The end is near!

She escapes into Oxford Street. In the opposite direction of the crowd she fights her way through. People pushing against her pressing against her. She jabs her way through a river of bodies, a dance of elbows and arms and knees. There is a commotion. She hears the clang of the Hare Krishnas approaching. They are pouring down the street a parade of tambourines and drums. They are gleeful children, men, women. They are carrying a wizened old man above their arms. They are dancing, clapping, singing. They are handing out plates of sweets to passersby. Tourists are stopping pointing taking their picture.

Hare Krishna Hare Krishna

Ruth turns the other way and begins to follow them, walking in the street. She is taken up by the masses. She is one of many. She is lost in the crowd.

(For wherever you go I will go…)

The end is near! The end is near! Her Oxford Circus preacher.

The crowd envelops her. More bodies, bodies, bodies. A shudder goes through her. She gasps for breath.

Hare Hare Hare

Save yourselves! Save yourselves!

An immense violence stirs inside her. A warmth. She fingers her tiny stub of a ponytail. Oh, to shave it all off. To be reborn. To be wiped clean.

(If I could smash that thing that houses me inside of myself.)

To disappear. A delirious death. She is drunk, dizzy with this sense of abandon. It is beginning to rain, a warm rain. The dingy day now thick with humidity. The robes of the Hare Krishnas dotted translucent. They form a circle. She doesn't know what she is doing. She is closing her eyes, she is throwing her arms up above her head, she is swaying back and forth, back and forth. She is dancing round and round. The ecstasy of the commotion.

(Such joy, such joy, such joy.)

I want to go to a church she thinks. I want to sit in a church and let the white light bathe me. It doesn't matter what church, what religion. It would be best if I did not understand the mumbling pleas directed up high. I want to go to a church and direct my eyes up high and open my arms up to the ceiling. And scream. And scream. And scream.

FIN

ACKNOWLEDGMENTS

Many thanks to: Cal Morgan at Harper Perennial, for taking a risk in republishing *Green Girl*, and for his edits helping me steward the novel into this revised P.S. edition. Marilyn Minter, for the use of her photograph for the cover. My agent Mel Flashman. Everyone else at HarperCollins. Those who helped support or shepherd *Green Girl* over the years in crucial ways, and all the passionate readers of the novel so far. Bryan Tomasovich for first publishing the novel at Emergency Press. And, as always, gratitude to my love, partner, and collaborator, John Vincler.

ABOUT THE AUTHOR

KATE ZAMBRENO is the author of two novels, *Green Girl* and *O Fallen Angel*, and of the nonfiction work *Heroines*, a memoiristic exploration of the wives and myths of the modernist movement. She teaches in the writing programs at Sarah Lawrence College and Columbia University.

Insights,
Interviews
& More . . .

About the author

About the book

Read on

The Allure of the Shopgirl

by Jessa Crispin

Meet Ruth. She's a little lost, a little feeble, a little unsteady on her feet. She is what Kate Zambreno, her creator, calls a Green Girl, a girl suffering through her own becoming. She is an American lost in London, working at a department store she bitterly calls Horrids, trying to force a perfume called Desire on American tourists.

You might not expect such a girl to keep the company of Walter Benjamin, Virginia Woolf, Joseph Cornell, and John Keats, but in Zambreno's world she does. Writers and filmmakers and philosophers weave in and out of her tale of one girl in danger of being gobbled by the big city. Her life might seem a little mundane, with the toing and froing on the London Underground, the dreary retail job, the boy problems and the girl problems and the hair problems. But the book is anything but. It cracks, it zings. It makes you call your girlfriend and read sections aloud over the phone. It makes you scribble down lines into a notebook, as Zambreno scribbled endless epigraphs into *Green Girl*.

I talked to Zambreno about Green Girls past and present, the pathos and delight of the department store, and why Virginia Woolf called on women writers to create fiction about the shopgirl.

Tell me a little about the shopgirl. All we know about her from the movies we've

seen her in is that she is delicate and poor, and desperately waiting for a man with money to save her from her circumstances.

Well to use a reference my cinephile-characters would love, the shopgirl in early film is also the vamp, the saucy flapper Clara Bow in *It* or the femme fatale Joan Crawford in *The Women*. And then, yes, there is the sad shopgirl-turned-hooker or manicurist-turned-hooker in a Godard film. But in film, even if these are films I adore and reference in the novel itself, the shopgirl mostly exists as a cipher, the glossy object of desire.

And yet Virginia Woolf in *A Room of One's Own* calls for the future woman writer to write the girl behind the counter. I have always been drawn to this girl sitting bored and waiting and have wanted to examine her life and livelihood as an object, as a becoming subject, how these two might tangle up in each other. What is the content of her interior monologue?

I see Ruth, my heroine, as a girl–Gregor Samsa whose consciousness is still dimmed and often dismissed, in life, in literature. Woolf writes of this too—that feminine experience is often rejected as not universal, hence not literary. There is, however, a literature of the shopgirl whose anti-heroines are the true ancestors of *Green Girl*—the Jean Rhys *jeune fille* in her between-the-war novels, Zelda Fitzgerald's girl portraits, Mary McCarthy's *The Company She Keeps*. I remember too what it was like to have no real sense of self, to be dull with flashes of brilliance, trying on jobs like hats. ▸

The Allure of the Shopgirl ***(continued)***

Harrods: The temple to girl consumer culture. You lived in London for a while; tell me what you thought about Harrods and why you selected it as the setting.

When I lived in London I was totally obsessed with the luxury department stores, how grand and impeccable they were, and as I was only there for a year I was in some way an utter tourist, and would spend my time being caught in the crowds on Oxford and Tottenham Court, just walking, getting lost, straining my neck to gaze at the horns on the top of Selfridges, saving up to have tea upstairs at Liberty, buying one little thing at the food hall at Harrods.

I also worked at Foyles Bookshop, beginning as a temp over the holiday season, and some of the characters and incidents are drawn from my experience there, the rush and the fatigue and the cliques. I found the experience of being a temp also to be revealing of my general experience as a foreigner, the second-class status, the dizzying sense of being temporary.

There are two department stores that feature heavily in the novel—Liberty and a store she merely refers to as Horrids. I liked the contradictory idea that Liberty was this place of utter *jouissance* and freedom for Ruth, that she went to on her day off, window-shopping so to speak like Holly Golightly at Tiffany's, while she viewed Horrids as this jail cell. I only went to Harrods a few times, but I found the place totally iconic but utterly vulgar, and also this ultimate tourist destination for

Americans, which I thought was kind of delicious. When I moved back to Chicago I would go often to the Marshall Field's on State Street. The perfume spritzer seemed the role with the most pathos.

I like that some of the saints show up as previous Green Girls. I always envied my friend's Catholic upbringing, because as a Methodist no one told me about St. Lucy. Tell me how that section came to live in the novel.

Yes, St. Lucy the ideal blonde who gives her beautiful blue eyes to her admirer, because she so wanted to distance herself from his gaze. It seems my childhood incubation in Catholicism always creeps into my works. Like so many Catholic little girls in their miniature wedding dresses, I was obsessed with the female saints. We read their lives in gold-plated prayer books—these mystics who felt intense loss and longing at His departure, and little Catholic girls too are trained to be madly in love with God.

Ruth to me is a mystic character, and much like these mystics she isn't looking for embodiment or empowerment but rather something closer to its opposite. She is searching for a form of decreation, an ecstasy that is outside of herself—she has sex, takes drugs, dances with Hare Krishnas, all in an attempt to find a higher level of experience.

I vampirized from these medieval confessions of intense girl-love for Ruth's prayer-like meditations on a past love affair. These meditations are threaded ▸

throughout the work (and are also inspired by Elizabeth Smart's channeling of the Song of Songs in *By Grand Central Station I Sat Down and Wept*). So my obsession with mysticism is throughout, but is explored in dialogue during the later scenes with the holy boy Ruth meets whom she longs to soil.

I am struck not only by the intensity of desire these women mystics felt, but also by how they weren't strictly authors of their own narratives but in fact always narrated their confessions to a male confessor who told their story for them. In my novel, the father-confessor is instead an ambivalent mother-narrator. A fantastic book I was reading during the height of writing was *Sensible Ecstasy*, Amy Hollywood's book about the obsession of the early twentieth-century French intelligentsia (Bataille, Simone de Beauvoir, Lacan) with Teresa of Avila and other mystics.

Ruth is sort of an exasperating but recognizable presence. You want both to slap her and to feed her like a baby bird. What did you think of her as you were writing?

I loved her. I felt great oozy empathy for her. I still do. There were many models for Ruth, but while writing the mass of the work in Chicago there was a girl who lived below me, an impossibly cool blonde, who I never had a conversation with, who cut her hair suddenly one day, and for a while I really modeled Ruth on her. I loved her, too.

Ruth is my past students and my past toxic friends and my own past as a toxic girl. I want Ruth to discover herself, to find herself, but also knew that I didn't want to create an easy or quick narrative of empowerment. But she is in that liminal state of being—she has not reached a real consciousness yet. It's infuriating. Ruth is often mean, petty, self-indulgent, impossibly vain, too tortured to live, passive. But she is also sensitive, a watcher of the world, a lover of beautiful things. So there is a glimmer, more than a glimmer, a possibility that Ruth will transcend being a character, my character, everyone's character, and become her own author. In some ways I think of the novel as an author and character in search of each other.

Jessa Crispin is the founder and editor-in-chief of Bookslut. *This interview first appeared in* Kirkus Reviews.

Notes Underground

The following are two scenes cut from the first edition of Green Girl.

At the time I wrote these basement scenes I was working on an essay on the British modernist Anna Kavan, whose dystopic texts explore the surveillance and hysteria of London during wartime. In Kavan's stories and novels a character is always without her papers, and everyone is vaguely the enemy. I think this Kavanesque paranoia suffuses these dreary underground sections, where Ruth works as a switchboard operator at Horrids, one of many temporary jobs she takes on and easily quits. Ultimately I took them out because I didn't think it was necessary to contribute to the atmosphere of tedium and boredom that was already conjured up in the Horrids sales scenes. But I am happy to see two short passages revived here, because I entirely forgot the character of Queasimodo, a nickname I am particularly fond of. And I had wanted to relate something about the bizarreness of an American girl answering the phones, expected to somehow perform Englishness, and how this accented even more her sense of surreality and foreignness.

I also missed the character nicknamed St. Louis: "She was one of those people you can never remember what they were wearing, as if they existed entirely from the neck up." The interactions between her and Ruth show a crucial other sort of underground among temporary service workers in London—Americans who try to pass, who desperately want to stay on, and the ambivalent fellowship between these reluctant citizens.

—K. Z.

The first scene is an alternative draft of the passage that begins on p. 172 of this edition.

Ruth, Ruth, I need you. Noncy appeared in front of her white and trembling as a ghost, as usual. Ruth and Ava Gardner had been chatting behind the counter leisurely. Ava Gardner was letting her try on her silver rings, which she clacked together.

You need to go down to the basement today.

Why? Ruth asked. Human resources was headquartered in the basement. She knew that this week her contract was expired and she would no longer be a temporary.

The expectation was that she would be hired on afterward. She wondered whether the fragrance department would keep her on, and secretly hoped they wouldn't. The terrible girls were not so terrible any longer, even Elspeth, but she couldn't stand being stationed so close to the outside. She braced herself with every cold whish of the door. But another part of her wished things would just remain the same, so she wouldn't have to be trained at anything new.

Noncy sighed impatiently. We need you to work in customer service today. All right? Today or forever? Was she being disentangled from The Italian and Ava Gardner? The undesirables sniffed out. Noncy sighed. I don't know Ruth. They've been expecting you. Ta! With a wave and a flurry she was off.

Ruth took the service lift downstairs to customer service. To get there she had to pass the luggage department. He was working today. The boy with the enflamed face. Again he looked like he had been waiting for her.

Rhys, was it? She wandered over to his area.

Yes, Ruth, right? They smiled at each other. Neither of them a great conversationalist.

You cut your hair.

Ruth nervously touched her head, as if startled to find it had disappeared in the middle of the night. Yeah. Change, I thought.

I like it. You look like Joan of Arc.

Thanks. Soft, breathy. ▸

Notes Underground ***(continued)***

How were your holidays?

Ruth winced. Oh, you know. She stared at her feet.

Are you all right, Ruth? Rhys asked, peering at her with a worried expression. He seemed so nice, so sensitive, such a nice boy.

I'm okay. Just, the holidays were . . . hard this year.

He nodded solemnly. Homesick?

Homesick? Ruth repeated. She felt again the ache of the tears starting to form. She wondered if the pain was palpable on her glossed face. Sick for something, I guess.

Would you like to have lunch sometime with me, Ruth? He looked serious, searching.

Yeah. Lunch. Okay.

Just then a balding, hunched-over man wearing a green vest came up to them. Ruth recognized him. She had seen him following after the horrible head, just one step behind. He carried the tired, worried air of a spinster. Are you the temp? he asked. Not anymore, Ruth said, knowing she was performing in front of Rhys. He waved his hand away hastily as if to dismiss her comment. Are you Ruth, then? he asked now with even more exasperation. She nodded. Well, we've been expecting you. Come on, let's go. Like pulling schoolchildren in single-file line. She followed after Queasimodo waving a quick goodbye to an ever-beaming Rhys.

They entered a room full of cubicles. Her heart sank. Is this where I will be serving my sentence? she thought. Forever barred from the above world of light and laughter and mirrors? A dozen pairs of bored reddened eyes swiveled when they walked in, and then swiveled back, satisfied somehow with what they saw. They remained hunched over their desks, all wearing the same dark green vest. Rows and rows of green after green, like a wholly felled forest.

We need help with the phones. Queasimodo directed her to an empty cubicle filled with debris and forgotten knick-knacks. She sat on an office chair of that indeterminate office-chair color. Is this my desk? Ruth asked. This is the desk you will be using. Anything else? All thoughts fled from Ruth's mind. Do I have to wear one of those? pointing at his green vest dotted with stains. He took this question seriously, as it concerned Horrids' hierarchy, and he was the kind to be always stern when dictating matters of dogma. No, that won't be necessary. Only those of us who deal directly with the public need to wear the vest. The Vest. Like it was an honor to wear.

As they stood there hovering above the desk, neither one of them sitting, a red light sounded on the dusty, sticky phone. Then another red. Then another. Soon the phone was crawling with a cacophony of lit-up buttons, the collective whine of an army of insects. The dozen pairs of eyes swiveled again at Ruth, annoyed.

You better answer that, Queasimodo said, then seemingly disappeared.

But I don't know what to say . . . she hesitated. She stood there frozen. The ringing.

Pick it up and greet them, a girl in glasses in the cubicle across from her finally piped up. Haven't you ever answered a telephone before?

Well, yes, but . . . She jabbed a finger at one of the red lights as if to kill it and then picked up the black receiver. Hello, she whispered. Hello, she repeated. The line was dead. Someone had hung up. She sat down. She tried another incessant red light. Hello. How can I help you? A pause at the other end. Yes, is this customer service for the store? Yes, yes, it is. I need to speak with someone, came an annoyed English voice on the other end. All right, one moment, let me put you on hold.

Umm, excuse me, sorry, Ruth whispered at the girl in glasses. She wants to speak with customer service. She seems angry. The girl sighed, annoyed as well. Well, give me a moment. She continued scribbling something on her piece of paper. Finally she looked up again. Well, who is it? I didn't get her name. Should I have? The girl sighs again. It's fine, I sup-pose. You can transfer her now. Just hit the transfer button and then type in my number, sixteen. Ruth did as she was told and released the phone like it was some live wriggling thing.

The girl picked up the phone. Her face smoothed out, lifted into a pleasant smile. The voice came out a soft perfect English. Good morning, how may I assist you?

Another red light sounded. Ruth pushed it in, picked up the phone, and tried to imitate her ease and friendliness. Good morning, how may I help you? Oh, Ladies? Designer? One moment. Let me put you on hold. How do I transfer to Ladies? Designer? She whispered panicked to the girl, who silently pointed her to a phone list on the wall next to Ruth's desk. Oh, okay, thanks. She whispered again. She didn't know why she was whispering. She pushed the button ▸

Notes Underground *(continued)*

back in. All right. I'm going to transfer you now. She pounded on the transfer button, then the number, and then hung up the phone, sighing with relief.

Thanks. She smiled at the girl who grimaced back, a thin line of veiled contempt, burying her head in her pile of papers on her desk. She had a black bob, like a sheet of black glass. I just kind of got thrown into this. There should be a training manual or something. The other girl shrugged her shoulders. Perhaps they were forbidden from socializing by Queasimodo. It's not rocket science, she responded, not with any meanness, but not with any friendliness either.

And this is how it went on all morning. Ruth begging for help, the reluctant girl with glasses coming to her rescue, until she was allowed to abandon her station at her lunch hour in search of some human warmth.

Queasimodo returns to the story in this second passage, originally appearing right after the phrase "... her solemn philosopher" on p. 203 of this edition.

It looks like we've got two of them now. Queasimodo stops in front of her cubicle. Hunched, over, balding, with the same beige sweater stretched over his shoulders. Every day that thin sweater hung a little lower. Ruth did not like him. He referred to his minions as children. All right, children, we're going to give it our all today.

Two of what? Ruth was confused.

Two Americans, he gestured at the girl with glasses and then at Ruth. We've got a set.

Ruth was in shock. You're American, she cried to the girl.

Yup. She nodded, curt as always. St. Louis.

Chicago, said Ruth. And that was all.

The inevitable exchange, breaking the code of silence amidst Americans abroad who preferred invisibility.

It looks like Ruth was supposed to be underground indefinitely.

Ruth found it strange that they would want an American girl to be the voice of Horrids, but no one else seemed to mind. Although those on the other end seemed perplexed until Ruth learned how to fake it. Good morning (good evening, good afternoon), how may

I direct your call? She would then transfer the call either to one of the departments at Horrids, or to one of the customer service representatives in the basement bent over worried in cubicles.

On the phone, every interaction carried its weight. The same weight. Ruth started to form shapes to the voices, like giving a personality to a chair.

At first everyone was a bit curious about her, once the basement dwellers knew she was going to stay for a while. Where did you come from? How did you get here? These were questions Ruth could not answer.

They grew used to her. That's what happens. People grow used to people, like setpieces that occasionally talk.

Even St. Louis grew used to her, although there was a remoteness, like she didn't want to get too close. She was one of those people you can never remember what they were wearing, as if they existed entirely from the neck up.

When the phone didn't ring Ruth sat at her desk and filed her nails. This was her playing the role of a switchboard operator. Sometimes she read.

Read on

Woman of the Crowd

Readings on *Flâneurs* and *Flâneuses*

WHILE WRITING *GREEN GIRL*, I was circling around **Walter Benjamin**'s section on the *flâneur*, or urban stroller, in his ***Arcades Project***, his catalogue/collage of the arcades of nineteenth-century Paris.

Walking. This is how I've started to think of writing. And thinking. Writing and thinking as walking.

Like other writers before me, I wondered how to resurrect a female walker in a contemporary urban space—what is her relationship to the gaze, she who is at once spectacle and also spectator (even specter?). Texts that conjure up for me the preferred Surrealist mood of *dépaysement*, a sort of induced displacement or disorientation, of seeing the world anew. The Canadian woman in **Gail Scott's *My Paris*** finding a copy of Benjamin's *Arcades Project* in her temporary Paris flat, she keeps a journal, in a syncopated, surprising rhythm, on her walks outside, on *flânerie*, on feeling foreign around the French. The wandering, meditative figures in the texts of **Renee Gladman** and **Pamela Lu**, moving through a lost or nostalgic city, both authors slyly bringing in other ideas of alterity and identity, of queerness and race as well. **Amina Cain**'s characters in her short stories, marveling through strange landscapes. **Danielle Dutton's S P R A W L**, which reads as if Gertrude Stein had channeled Alice B. Toklas writing an *Arcades Project* set in an absurd suburbia.

The pilgrimage of **Kathy Acker**'s girl fuckup in ***Don Quixote***. Acker's Lousy

Mindless Salesgirl Janey Smith in ***Blood and Guts in High School***, traveling from Mexico to working in a vegan bakery in the East Village to becoming the property of a Persian slave trader to trailing about Algiers after a sadistic Jean Genet.

Jane Bowles's deliriously odd mystics in ***Two Serious Ladies***, finding an intoxication amidst the masses like Edgar Allan Poe's story "The Man of the Crowd," which Benjamin pivots around. Bowles's characters entranced by seediness, by slumming. (Her obsession with prostitutes, whom Benjamin also links with the walker in *The Arcades Project*.) Mrs. Copperfield lost and stumbling in Panama City, striking up accidental and ambivalent relationships with other women. She becomes voyeur. The erotics of witnessing as opposed to being witnessed. Marguerite Duras' housewife-*fuguer* in ***The Ravishing of Lol Stein***, the object of obsession, watched over through the entire work by the narrator. She is a minor celebrity in town, a subject of gossip, walking around town in a state of amnesiac unconsciousness. This, too, is something she escapes from in her fugue states. Like **Djuna Barnes**'s Robin Vote in ***Nightwood***, on her nighttime walks, escaping the oppressiveness of her past, the oppressiveness of being the beloved, escaping being a character. The cipher-somnambule leaves her body, the scene of the crime. Erika Kohut in **Elfriede Jelinek**'s ***The Piano Teacher***, surveyed by an oppressive mother, escaping into peepshows and pickup spots at night to spy on others. Nightvision. Lol Stein surrendering herself deliriously in a field of rye. Erika K. squatting by the tree, a trickle of urine down her leg.

I am drawn too to the texts of female drifters, those who disappear or are never really seen. Vagabondes and demimondes. Reading Baudelaire, Benjamin envisions the *flâneur* as overcome and intoxicated with empathy. Sasha Jensen in **Jean Rhys**'s ***Good Morning, Midnight***, a woman in public, feeling the pain of belonging nowhere, of being stared at, of being ignored. Rhys's character is stripped of that skin of indifference one needs in order to exist in public, away from prying eyes. But she is overcome with feelings too—brought on by memories of Paris, a city she has returned to, temporarily, to that street, that shop where she once worked, feelings for the balding older lady with the mean daughter trying on hats, feelings for the charismatic con artists who get by preying on the rich. Another vagabonde, the old lady in **Violette Leduc**'s ***The Little Lady in the Fox Fur***, hungry, poor, finding mystic value and meaning in objects. ▸

Woman of the Crowd *(continued)*

I have also been inspired by films of the walker, the drifter. The opening of **Barbara Loden**'s 1970 film ***Wanda***, Loden a wraithlike figure in white, making her way slowly, slowly, through mountains of coal. Wanda like the drifter played by Sandrine Bonnaire in **Agnès Varda**'s 1985 film ***Vagabond***, called in French *Sans toit ni loi* (Without roof or law). Wanda wanders into a Mexican cinema and falls asleep, only to wake and find her wallet gone.

Agnès Varda's earlier ***Cléo from 5 to 7*** (1962), her pop-star blonde played by Corinne Marchand, wandering through the streets, aware of the gaze of others, never alone and yet always alone, trying on hats like confections in the mirror. But what Varda was trying to perform, or critique, about the character, is really interesting—turning the object of desire into a subject, a meditation, a subjective documentary, of a woman in city streets, who can never be completely anonymous. Varda was inspired by **Rainer Maria Rilke**'s ***The Notebooks of Malte Laurids Brigge***, but in that work Brigge can be invisible; he can blend in as he walks around la Salpêtrière, unlike Varda's heroine.

Since *Green Girl* was the first novel I ever attempted to write, there was a wandering to its creation too, to the process of invention and discovery. And my Ruth, my Ruth wanders too, through her gray city, propelled by horror and ecstasy in the crowd. Ruth wanders, uncertain of whether she wants to be found.

—K. Z., January 2014

Don't miss the next book by your favorite author. Sign up now for AuthorTracker by visiting www.AuthorTracker.com.